SIREN SONG

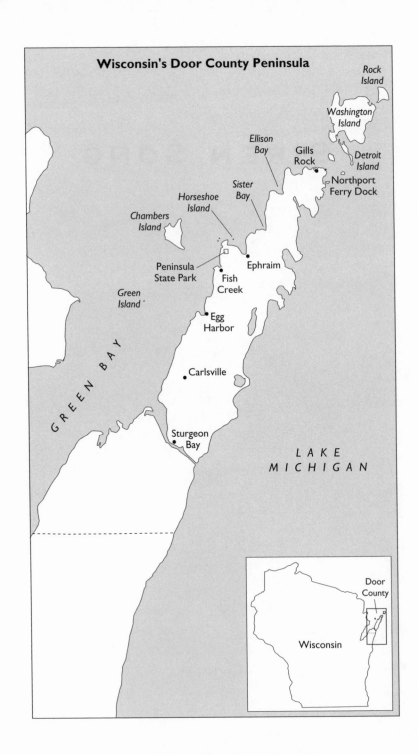

Wisconsin's Door County Peninsula

Rock Island

Washington Island

Detroit Island

Ellison Bay

Gills Rock

Northport Ferry Dock

Sister Bay

Horseshoe Island

Chambers Island

Peninsula State Park

Ephraim

Fish Creek

Green Island

Egg Harbor

Carlsville

Sturgeon Bay

GREEN BAY

LAKE MICHIGAN

Door County

Wisconsin

SIREN SONG

A SUSPENSE NOVEL

STEPHEN SCHWANDT

BRIDGE WORKS PUBLISHING COMPANY

Bridgehampton, New York

Published by Bridge Works Publishing Company, Bridgehampton, New
York, an imprint of The Rowman & Littlefield Publishing Group, Inc.

Distributed in the United States by National Book Network, Lanham,
Maryland. For descriptions of this and other Bridge Works books, visit the
National Book Network website at www.nbnbooks.com.

FIRST EDITION

The characters and events in this book are fictitious. Any similarity to actual
persons, living or dead, is coincidental and not intended by the author.

For more information on the author, see his website at
www.StephenSchwandt.com.

Library of Congress Cataloging-in-Publication Data

Schwandt, Stephen.
    Siren song : a suspense novel / Stephen Schwandt.— 1st ed.
      p. cm.
    ISBN 1-882593-89-8 (hardcover : alk. paper) — ISBN 1-882593-88-X
(pbk. : alk. paper)
    1. Door County (Wis.)—Fiction. 2. Boats and boating—Fiction. 3.
Police corruption—Fiction. I. Title.

    PS3569.C5645S57 2004
    813'.54—dc22

            2004004730

10 9 8 7 6 5 4 3 2 1

∞™ The paper used in this publication meets the minimum requirements
of American National Standard for Information Sciences—Permanence of
Paper for Printed Library Materials, ANSI/NISO Z39.48–1992.
Manufactured in the United States of America.

For Karen, again and always

With special thanks to Norb Blei,
generous mentor and friend;
Kate Benson and Dan Schultz,
young writers to watch

"So many give up so much so soon for so little."
—Nelson Brite, *Appropriations*

SIREN SONG

CHAPTER 1

"Hey man, this is borrrr-*ing*," Jerry Woodrow complained. "*Real* boring."

I was trying to get the class focused, a discussion started.

"Jerry," I said, "it's Friday. This is the last unit of the semester. School ends in a week . . ." Was I pleading?

"Aw, c'mon, Mr. Griffin," Jerry persisted. "*Old Man and the* freakin' *Sea*?! That's the best you got?"

Jerry—chubby, blond, fifteen—was your typical average student in any section of regular American Lit 10 at Hoover High School in suburban Minneapolis.

"It's true, Jerry," I continued, "that this little book has been called Hemingway's best story, while other critics have called it his most overrated work. And the story does take place a long time ago in a country and culture that's obviously very different from ours. But the story might still be worthwhile to study today, right now. Why might—?"

"What's to *study*?!" cut in Bethany Slater, the much-pierced, purple-haired, runway-model-thin captain of Row 6. "Old guy goes for the big one and loses big. End of story."

"Is it really that simple?" I said. "Could the fish be more than a fish? The fisherman more than just another fisherman?"

"Ohhhh, *no*!" blurted Tremain Evans, one of eight black students in the class. He was both a very promising wide receiver in football and the top candidate to win this semester's Most Improved Player Award in American Lit.

"*Oh no* to what, Tremain?"

"No more symbols, man. Looks like where you're headed."

"Well, Hemingway himself remarked that if you find symbols in his fiction, you can make of them what you want. His job, he said, was to write the stuff, not lead guided tours through it."

"There you go," said Tremain, nodding. "So let's just relax and enjoy, huh?"

"But in a speech he wrote when he won the Nobel Prize for literature," I continued, "Hemingway described a writer as someone who is driven far out past where he should go, out to where no one can help him. Who else is described that way? Who describes himself that way?"

"Santiago," said Amy Nguyen. "The old man."

"So writers are fishermen now?!" scoffed Jerry Woodrow.

"No metaphors either!" called out Tremain, staring hard at me.

Laughter rippled across the room.

I tried again. "Suppose I asked you to explore that parallel—writers as fishermen. What are some other things Santiago says about himself that a writer might say?"

Tremain started with, "Over and over, the old man talks about keeping his lines straight. Cat's always bein' precise, exact, deep."

"He's talking about a *fishing* line, T," said Jerry. "That's all. It's just a freakin' fish-that-got-away story."

"Writers try to keep their thoughts straight, too," replied Tremain, cool and calm. "Which you might wanna try someday, Woody."

"But what's really the subject of the story?" I pressed. Except for the few participating, the rest of the class seemed far far away.

"'This is a tale of courage, endurance, pride, humility, and death,'" said Jerry, reading a blurb from the book cover.

"Thanks for sharing, Wood-man," said Tina Yates, sitting right behind Jerry. She paused from fixing her nail polish to pat him on the shoulder.

"Let me put it this way," I continued, although I knew the threshold to genuine interest would remain uncrossed. "Literature is news that *stays* news. So, what's *the news* here in this book? What's the truth, if you will, that could mean something in your lives?"

Before Jerry Woodrow could come up with another wiseass comment, Rachel Quinn slowly raised her hand, the first student to do so. Rachel had had a tough semester, caught in the midst of her parents' bitter divorce.

"Yes, Rachel?"

The class fell wholly silent, atypically silent.

"Maybe what Hemingway wants to tell us is that sooner or later we're all going to try for some big success, some big prize. But sometimes, even when you do everything the right way and you deserve to succeed, the prize isn't what you thought it would be. Or you might have the prize a while but lose it."

"What's that got to do with fishermen being the same as writers?" asked Jerry, smirking. I wanted to grab his blond mop and bounce his face on the desk.

"Woody," said Tremain, twisting around to face him, "why don't you zip it, man? Do some thinkin' for a change. Girl's *sayin' something*, you know?"

But before anyone could extend our discussion in any direction, the fire alarm sounded and even I was drowned out by the grating whine of Hoover's new pulsating "Synchronized-Alert Siren System Escape Enhancer."

The class shuffled dutifully out of the room, heading for the exits and the seductive promise of saying goodbye to E. Hemingway and his lessons in exchange for a bright late-spring morning.

"*Outside!*" I hollered needlessly, then trailed my kids to our designated safe spot set up exactly two hundred feet from the building.

On my way out I ran into my hall duty partner and favorite ally on the faculty, Kevin Vesical. Like me, Kevin was single again and in his early thirties, but he looked much younger than his age, perpetually handsome in a dark-haired soap-opera-star way. Prime-time Alec Baldwin with a close shave. And like Baldwin, Vesical was a theater guy—our very successful drama coach and play director. During his ten years at Hoover, he'd already won so many awards for the school in his specialty that there were hardly any left to win.

I asked him, "Was this a scheduled drill?"

"*Scheduled*?!" He slapped his left palm to the side of his head, eyes popping. "You mean like somebody's actually *in charge* here? C'mon, JP."

"What was I thinking?" I muttered, stepping into the blissful sunlight, joining our students across the lawn,

ready to drop down right there in the lush grass myself,
nod off, call it a day.

Eventually, the howling Synchronized-Alert Siren System
Escape Enhancer stopped, the familiar return bell
sounded, and the reluctant forced march back into the
labyrinthian confines of Hoover High began. I knew my
class was hoping Ernest Hemingway wouldn't return.

In front of my classroom door, a scrawny little guy with
spiky, streaked hair, wearing a black T-shirt announcing
the *COCK-SURE SUMMER TOUR*, was pinning a young
girl against the locked door I needed to open. With a fore-
arm on the girl's neck, nearly lifting her off the floor, and
with his free hand under her skirt, he was playing grab-ass,
while she squealed with perverse delight.

Standing directly behind the kid, I said, "Okay, my man,
let's relax, huh? I have to open up."

He ignored my request, trying now to kiss the giggling
girl.

"You *hear* me?!" I said much louder, leaning closer. No
response.

By now the hall traffic had slowed, the mob sensing the
start of a *scene*, something to write notes about in home-
room.

Placing my open right hand on the boy's upper right
arm, the arm of his tickling hand, I began gently but
firmly to ease him aside. And that's when he turned on
me, throwing up his arm and knocking my hand away,
hollering, "Get your fuckin' hands offa me, you *fuck*!"

The hall traffic gridlocked, then began inching closer,
too close for my comfort.

"What's your name?" I asked.

"Don't need my name, you *fuck*! Chill out, huh?" He stuck his bony chest at me and belched in my face.

Truly, I wanted to end it right there. Deck this punk and drag him to the office, maybe heave him right through the front door. Instead, I jammed my fists in my pants pockets, my left hand finding my laminated faculty photo ID card, which I began to flick with the edge of my thumb. This ID badge was supposed to be clipped to my shirt or hung from a lanyard around my neck, but I felt stupid wearing the damn thing, so I kept it in my pocket. Maybe this rude kid didn't realize I was certified faculty.

"You know what *insubordination* is?" I finally responded.

"Fuck off!"

"Probably can't find his ass with both hands," said Tremain Evans, trying to help.

"Look man, I found *mine*!" piped up the tickled girl at my other elbow. She was clutching her buttocks and getting a raucous guffaw from the closest observers, and another "Dumb fuck!" from her boyfriend, directed at me, of course.

And to Evans, the kid said, "Go sniff a jockstrap or something."

Before the two could mix it up, the boy hollered to the crowd, "Fuckin' guy laid *hands* on me! Fuckin' threw me against the fuckin' *wall*!" Then to me, "Gonna fuckin' *pay* for that, dude!"

Before the day was over, I received a note of apology from "Nick" saying: "I shunta told you to fuckoff. So sorry." Along with that came his counselor's memo telling me that I had "response documents" to complete before the final bell. I was also informed by this counselor that "the unfortunate victim in your needlessly confrontational misunderstanding, Nicholas Cassalato, is really a bright young man who is working hard in group to come to terms with such problems as properly socializing his anger management skills, while at the same time diffusing his stress-induced feelings of failure ideation."

I'd already learned from Vesical that Nick had recently been charged with beating up an elderly aunt to get "smokin' money."

"What's he doing in school?" I asked Kevin.

"Case pending" was the explanation.

But there it was on *my* plate—a full helping of the Terrible Truth for Today's Teachers: Our authority has been so completely undermined by micro-managing educrats that we can't correct student dress, language, or behavior without violating their "rights," while our students have been convinced that being happy and well adjusted in school is far more important than facing the stressful challenge of significant academic work. As a classroom instructor, I was sick of being told what to do by people who didn't seem to do anything very well.

When that long, terminally disenchanting school day finally ended, I grabbed my briefcase and a plastic bag full of ungraded themes and literally *ran* for the parking lot, piling quickly into my Jeep Wrangler. Once midnight blue, now fading from a rough 162,000 miles of wear, the Wrangler headed in the *opposite* direction from home. I knew then that I couldn't remain in the classroom and still believe I was teaching—that I was truly motivating my students to challenge every day their own potential for intellectual improvement. Like nearly all of my colleagues, I had made too many bad treaties with my students: *If you behave and let me pretend I'm teaching, I'll pretend you're learning and pass you.* Now, I could no longer expect, let alone demand, anything more from these kids than the mindless mediocrity my administration wanted from me.

I didn't go back to my crappy bachelor apartment in southwest Minneapolis. Instead, I drove east, straight to Wisconsin, racing toward Green Bay, the Door County Peninsula, Lake Michigan.

I hadn't packed a thing, not even a toothbrush. I had perhaps $100 in cash and enough credit-card buying power to get me through the weekend. I was fed up and fleeing my life. But with my luck, this weekend Cock-Sure would be playing a sold-out mega-concert at Lambeau Field, and Nick Cassalato would be in the crowd, standing front row center, drunk and high, exposing himself, spitting on the cops, and screaming that his name was JP Griffin.

CHAPTER 2

Soon, I was crossing the wide St. Croix, a sparkling wave-rippled and already boat-crowded stretch of recreational waterway that separates Minnesota and Wisconsin. Then I found myself winding and turning, rising and falling over western Wisconsin, concentrating on the freeway as it sometimes slashed through hillsides, sometimes swept around them, sometimes shot straight into wide-open stretches of comforting, wonderfully symmetrical, meticulously maintained farmsteads and fields and forests.

A long six hours from now, at the other end of the newly refurbished Highway 29, I would be on the Lake Michigan shore, a place I'd been as happy as I'll probably ever be. There, in a small coastal town sixty miles south of Door County, I had grown up, an only child, my dad a history teacher and coach. My mother had been born, raised, and educated in Manette, and worked her whole life there as the town librarian.

It had been nearly nine years since I'd last been on the "thumb" of Wisconsin, that vacation area of my youth, with its thick forests and wide beaches. The limestone peninsula jutted northeast some eighty miles into Lake Michigan, a land of wind and water and capricious weather, the site of over two hundred shipwrecks, a place I'd almost wrecked for myself about five years earlier by bringing my ex-wife Margot there to unwind for a few days after our European honeymoon. I floored the Wrangler and shot past a motorhome I'd been tailing for maybe ten miles. Almost any recollection of Margot had that effect on me now, the urge to let loose, break free.

Nearing Shawano, I pulled into a rest stop to use the men's room. Even though the coffee I bought had delivered the energizing jolt I'd needed, all that had gone unabsorbed was now lobbying for release. Washing up, I stared empty-eyed at my drawn face with its fresh stubble. I was a wreck. I stayed in the lav for only a few minutes but when I reemerged, I discovered that afternoon was rather suddenly turning to evening.

Just outside Green Bay, Wisconsin, the sun disappeared along with most of my visibility. A massive wall of fog had come drifting in off Lake Michigan, covering the landscape, darkening the sky, chilling the air, and nearly obliterating the roadway and exit signs. The beautiful early June day had disappeared along with the warm nostalgia I'd conjured up. Only at the last possible moment was I able to make out the exit marker showing me where to take a left turn and catch Highway 41 north. Soon I exited again to begin driving a stretch of freeway that quickly became the arcing, 120-foot-high, four-lane, mile-long Tower Drive Bridge, which spanned the Fox River, right where it joined the waters of Green Bay.

In a misty silence, I approached the bridge crest, hugging the inside shoulder. No sooner had I cleared the crest than a car, a dark sedan, barreled toward me in the oncoming lane, riding so close to the centerline barrier and me that my breath caught in my throat. A woman driver, with a plain white M on her door. A company car?

Then, just behind the sedan, roof lights flashing, a Green Bay police cruiser, also crowding the centerline, hurled itself in my direction. The cop at the wheel slowed his car when we passed each other, and for a split second the curtains of fog parted just long enough for us to stare at one another dead-on, and then . . . *Whoosh*, he vanished. I remembered the cop's face—handsome and square-jawed, but tense with annoyance or fear.

Close behind the cop, a battered light-colored pickup truck hammered along in pursuit. Then silence, more fog, a continuing descent, and only one more set of oncoming headlights to worry about before I could be safely off the bridge. Those headlights rode high and wide, belonging to a huge semi rig. But the truck and trailer huffed past without incident and finally I was back on level ground. The fog continued to pile up, surging like a snowstorm.

Within an hour I arrived at the southern outskirts of Sturgeon Bay. No longer was there an "off season" in Door County. May was barely over and two festivals were already in progress. Motels were full. Luckily, I spotted a little ma-and-pa motel, The Wayfarer Haven, ten or twelve cement-block units, and a lit VACANCY sign. Inside the small office, I found a trim, neat, 60-something man hunched at a desk behind the check-in counter. He wore a plaid cotton shirt and tan slacks, everything about him looking crisp.

"Hi. I'd like a room for tonight and probably tomorrow night, too."

The old guy looked up, smiled pleasantly and nodded, then reached for a room key on the panel of hooks behind him.

"And what's the best marina around here?" I asked. "I mean, the one with the biggest selection of boats, best prices, warranties, all that?" A plan of therapeutic action was rapidly taking shape in my head.

The old man stared kindly at me above the top of his reading glasses. He glanced over at an older woman at a tiny desk off in the corner, also bespectacled, also with the same closely cropped thick gray hair, also plaid-shirted, but wearing a long light blue denim skirt. "Maybe somebody for Kriel, eh Mother?" he asked.

Husband and wife? They could have been brother and sister.

The bright-eyed woman looked up from her work, gave her husband a wink and warm smile, then nodded once at me with absolute certainty.

"What's the name again?" I asked.

"Wally Kriel," answered the man. "Wally 'The Deal' Kriel."

I thanked the couple, glancing once more around the office area, paneled in knotty pine, the walls covered with family photos of fishing and boating and picnic scenes. All I carried in the way of luggage was a paper bag of basics I had bought at a convenience store—toothbrush, tooth-paste, razor, shaving cream, some snacks. The old man eyed my bag of purchases.

"Traveling kinda light, eh?"

"Like a refugee."

The motel owner squinted, as though he were trying to determine whether I was serious. Then he leaned back in his swivel chair and laced his hands behind his head.

I spotted a stack of guidebooks at the end of the counter and picked one up. I also discovered a small rack of Wayfarer Haven business cards so I grabbed one of those too. "You mind?" I asked.

"That's why they're there."

What my host didn't know was that over the last few years I'd become business card *obsessed*, taking them wher-ever they were offered, even when there wasn't a chance in hell I'd ever make use of them. I started doing this when Margot, my ex, gave me a business card from her new job. If she was trying to initiate me, she succeeded. The cards would accumulate in my left pants pocket until I had a small deck to shuffle during those nervous times when my left hand needed something to do.

Eventually, the cards became limp and unresponsive. Then I'd pull them out, toss them all, and start another col-lection. So now The Wayfarer's card joined my card-size fac-ulty badge, Margot's severely damaged but kept-together-by-tape card, and several other recent acquisitions—cards from a textbook salesman, a financial analyst, a dentist, a barber, a Wausau gas station.

"Well, g'night," I said, heading out to my room, number 12, end unit. And I quickly discovered that I was the very last wayfarer to be granted shelter on this disturbing, dis-orienting night. The fog had settled in, deepening like a shroud. All the other units showed dim lights through drawn drapes. And all had an SUV or minivan parked directly in front of each numbered entrance, the vehicles piled high with top-carriers or bicycles or canoes or kayaks.

When I had unlocked the door to my room and flipped on the light, I sat down on the bed, ate half a bag of pretzels, and downed a can of 7-Up. I glanced around and took in the nautical decorating—the lighthouse-shaped lamp, the framed prints of schooners and clipper ships at sea, the pale blue bedspread dotted with little white anchors and red ship's wheels. I leaned back on the bed and fell asleep in my clothes.

In the dead of night I woke up long enough to undress, wash my face and return to the comfortable bed. I pulled down the covers and crawled back into a deep and very satisfying sleep, comforted by the familiar rhythmic moan of an area foghorn, just like when I was a kid. I dreamed that Tremain and Nick were wrestling with a cop on a fog-entombed bridge.

CHAPTER 3

I woke to a sunny, nearly cloudless sky and soothing warm breeze. The fog had dissipated, and so had my gloom. I decided that I would go back to face my last week of the spring semester at Hoover, then request an unpaid leave of absence for the coming fall semester. Even though I liked many of my students, I didn't like most of them. Even though I needed the money teaching would provide, I needed my freedom more. So I would next gather my savings, return to Door County, buy a boat, and live out a fantasy that had fascinated me since grade school. During my childhood I spent far too much time staring out classroom windows at Lake Michigan, following the progress of any vessel in view—a colorful sloop, expensive powerboat, or sooty freighter.

But it wasn't just *my* fantasy, this endless summer of cruising. It had also been a dream of my old man. For years when I was a kid, he had talked about buying a big boat and touring the Lake Michigan shoreline "top to bottom, left to right." He'd even purchased small pieces of nautical equipment that he planned to install aboard his dream vesssel once he'd gathered sufficient funds to sponsor such an expedition. I still had his marine compass (an anachronism in this age of GPS navigation), along with his illuminated chart-reading magnifier, his bright yellow, waterproof nylon sou'wester and hat, his solid-brass ship's bell complete with wall-mount brackets. And many evenings, instead of grading his students' tests and papers, my dad would page through boating magazines, searching the yacht broker listings for the perfect power cruiser. Unfortunately, he never could find the money or the time to realize his plans. So my tour, should I get to have one, would be made in his honor.

I decided to become a "live-aboard" on my own yacht and spend the summer in thoughtful isolation, cruising the area waters. The $36,857.00 inheritance finally released to me after my dad's death was hardly a fortune but still a tidy sum, especially for a man in the teaching field. Personally, I never expected a penny from my parents. Life for them was economically stressful even before my father died, more stressful than I ever knew. I learned too late that they'd refinanced their house to cover Mom's soaring medical expenses. She had lupus and everyone expected her to die way before my dad. But she didn't.

It happened right in our front yard. My father had been working under his ten-year-old Ford Escort sedan, the front wheels of the Escort being held aloft by two "slightly used" steel ramps he'd recently purchased through a newspaper ad. But one of the ramps collapsed, dropping the car on my father, killing him instantly. The closed-casket funeral ended in a fine needle rain.

But if I spent that $36,000 this summer and ran out of cash too soon, I would resign from Hoover and take another teaching job right here in Wisconsin. Teachers in my age group no longer had lucrative state retirement options to protect, or loyalty-inducing benefit packages that tied them to any particular school district. We were now "independent contractors," with all the "risks and responsibilities" typical of that job status. The superintendent in my school district called this "an enhanced options approach to labor relations."

So it wasn't teaching itself I wanted to flee. It was teaching at Hoover High, a school named for J. Edgar Hoover, the longtime, cross-dressing, control-freak director of the FBI. Other schools could not possibly be run so incompetently. Where else would an administration enact a "bomb threat strategy" that directed all staff and students to gather in the unlockable gym and "wait there until further notice"?

After a shave and shower, I reluctantly dressed myself in the same rumpled and clammy clothes I'd lived in for the past twenty-four hours. A large spot of soda decorated my shirt. Then, over breakfast at the Captain's Galley, one of the area's many privately owned restaurants (franchise eateries are discouraged in Door County), I promptly lost all sense of well-being when I flipped open the *Green Bay Bulletin* and spotted a page two story entitled *LOCAL PO-LICE OFFICER KILLED IN FOG*. The article reported:

> *Charles J. Parnell, a thirteen-year veteran of the Green Bay City Police Force, plunged to his death last evening when his patrol car was rear-ended and pushed off the Tower Drive Bridge. The extremely dense fog blanketing*

the area is thought to be a key factor in the accident. After the fog thinned late last night, rescue workers aided by police divers were able to retrieve the car from 25 feet of water with Officer Parnell's body still inside. An autopsy has been ordered.

According to sources, Officer Parnell, driving in the westbound lane of I-43, lost control of his vehicle, which was subsequently struck by a fully loaded semi rig driven by Victor Colby of Two Rivers, who was uninjured. In preliminary reports, Colby claims that he never saw Parnell's car before the moment of impact. But Colby also asserts that the squad car "was already skidding way up against the wall" seconds before the accident.

It occurred to me as I read that the officer I'd observed last night had activated his roof lights but not his siren, making the cruiser a sort of blinking ghost ship.

I continued reading:

Less than an hour before the accident, Officer Parnell made his last contact with the police dispatcher, when he called in to report that he was "initiating pursuit of a dented older model pickup truck, light in color, with Green Bay Packers logos painted on both cab doors." Parnell had continued: "The subject vehicle is being driven erratically, and it looks like there's kegs of beer and two or three intoxicated young men riding in the open truckbed."

The story went on to explain Parnell's connection to the University of Wisconsin–Green Bay campus, and how well respected he was there by both students and staff, and how effectively he dealt with the drunk-and-disorderly case he was investigating yesterday. The article ended by announcing:

> *Funeral arrangements for Charles Parnell have yet to be finalized. At the time of his death he was single with no children and no local next of kin. The investigation into his death is not yet complete.*

My breathing became shallow. Charles J. Parnell must have been the cop I'd exchanged startled glances with the night before. All the specifics I'd observed were mentioned in the article, but the vehicle order didn't seem right. I mean, there was no mention of the dented light-colored pickup truck I'd seen *following* Parnell. And I couldn't recall any Packers logo on the cab door of that truck, a detail that might implicate the frat boys in some ill-conceived revenge plot. I suppose I could've missed the logo. The truck was far from clean. And what about the woman in the company car Parnell seemed to be pursuing? I wondered if I should report my observations to the authorities. If I did call the police or the newspaper, what exactly would I report? How sure could I be of what I thought I saw? The fog had been so thick and swirling. How helpful would my information prove?

Still . . .

I left the restaurant determined to regain my focus and do what I'd come here to do—look for a boat, a cabin cruiser, a small efficient neat space that I could control. I needed a new lifestyle and, for that matter, a new life. But first I needed to make a phone call. I needed to do the right thing.

Finding a public booth just outside the restaurant, I dialed the Green Bay Police Department. When the desk clerk answered, I began: "About that cop Parnell who died last night? I think I passed by him going in the opposite direction just before he got hit."

"And your name is?"

"I'd rather not say."

"Sir, it's policy that—"

"What you should know," I continued, "is I think the newspaper story is wrong. Parnell passed by me with his light bar on and his siren off. He was following a car with an M on the driver's side door. Then close behind him came an old pickup truck, beige or yellow, and finally the semi. There were no Green Bay Packers logos on the truck I could see. And the semi was well back of both the squad car and truck."

"Listen, we need you to come in and make a full statement, okay?"

"That *is* my full statement," I said, hanging up quickly, my breathing ragged.

I stood there a few moments longer to collect myself. I didn't want to become more involved. I wanted to step *away* from involvement.

CHAPTER 4

Wally Kriel's office was clearly visible as I drove into the marina complex. A huge red-lettered sign proclaiming "HEY FRIEND, LET'S DEAL!" stood over the metal door of a small trailer-like outbuilding sitting on a cement-block foundation close to the water's edge. In the office, a middle-aged woman looking secretarial—pleasantly plump, short, curly brown hair, a phone tucked between her ear and shoulder as she leaned over her computer keyboard, scanning the screen through horn-rimmed half-glasses, saying "Uh-huh . . . Uh-huh, we got that part in stock, Bob. Really. Hey, I'm looking at it right now—the Harken Standard Winch #8 . . . yeah, in bronze. Two of 'em." When she looked up and noticed me, she said to Bob, "Just a sec, sweetie." And to me: "Yes? Can I help you?"

I asked, "Is Mr. Kriel in today?"

Before she could answer, a deep voice called out from somewhere down a short corridor to my left: "You catch one of my TV ads?"

I was about to reply: "Uh . . . no . . ." when there he was in front of me—Wally "The Deal" Kriel, celebrity salesman and marina owner, a smiling, burly, gray-bearded, balding man, dressed in stained khaki work pants and a loose-fitting blue sweatshirt with the sleeves cut off at the elbows. His pale eyes glittered at me from behind small steel-rimmed glasses, which Kriel pulled off and promptly put back on, a mannerism repeated many times during our subsequent conversations.

I said, "Word of mouth. Word on the street."

Kriel's grin widened. "*Referral!*" he boomed with relish. "Who?"

"Whoever runs The Wayfarer Haven, nice old guy and his wife, I think."

"Jens and Gert!" Kriel clapped his thick strong hands together just once. "Sold him and his sons seven . . . no, eight boats through the years."

"So he's loyal."

"Helluva guy, really. But who're you?"

"JP Griffin." I extended my hand.

Which Kriel engulfed with his heavily callused grip and pumped hard once. "My pleasure," said Kriel. "You know I never forget a name."

"Is that right?"

"Handy in this business."

"I bet."

"You wanna know something about Jens?" Wally Kriel grabbed my elbow and held it. "He's kept that motel in the black for nearly thirty-five years. Not many people around here can say that about a small, family-owned business, especially lodging."

"Uh-huh."

"I mean, I wouldn't kid ya," Kriel continued his recitation, leading me outside. "Places come and go, open and close, but Jens . . . he'll hang on forever. You know why? Cuz he's also kept a customer base that's so loyal they still stay with him even *after* they get rich enough to buy from me! Hah! That's a joke, okay? Now, what're you interested in?"

"Well, I want a big enough cabin cruiser to live aboard by myself, but not so big that I'd have trouble learning to operate and handle the thing, or finding dockage in the Door County area," I said, thankful we had finally got the subject back to boats.

"Explorin' the lake this summer, are ya? Short-range cruising, tie up for a few days at a time, sightsee, like that?"

"Pretty much exactly. A floating cottage is what I'm after."

Kriel directed his gaze out over his vast stock. "New or used?"

"Used, probably."

"Then what's your price range?"

There I was stumped. I'd come to Kriel on faith alone. I hadn't taken the time to research any particular boat, hadn't determined what a fair price would be for what I thought I wanted and needed, what brand, layout, engine configuration I preferred. I knew nothing at all really about cabin cruisers. I was completely out of my depth.

"Limited funds?" prompted Kriel.

"There're limits, but I've got cash," I explained. My attention was suddenly drawn to a nice-looking motor yacht just across the boat basin. "What do you want for something like that?" I asked.

"The Thompson?"

"I guess. The one with the taller cabin."

Kriel gave me another bemused once-over and asked, "You familiar with boats like that?"

"If you were standing right next to me calling out step-by-step instructions, I might be able to start the thing up."

Kriel chuckled. "Good enough," he said, encouragingly. "Cuz I hate the bullshitters that sometimes wander in here. But I'll take good care of you." He seemed to mean it, this garrulous local. But he had been touted as always making a deal, no mattter what.

"I mean," Kriel went on, gesturing at the entire marina, "you wouldn't believe what's happened here a few times. Guys who jump aboard, turn the key, and plow right into whatever's closest, thinking they're on *Baywatch* or some other goddam TV show! Just slam 'er into gear and rip! No skill or preparation or experience needed, right? Just jam the throttle full speed ahead! But you're not like that, are you."

"I'll take advice." Was this guy in his overheated speech really checking me out?

"Good attitude." Looking back again at the vessel in question, Kriel said, "That's a twenty-nine-foot Adventurer, eight years old. Got twin Merc two-sixties, full galley, flybridge with all the covers, swim platform, bow pulpit, a helluva nice boat. It'll run you $45,000."

"Holy *shit*," I let slip, looking away, my twitchy left hand going to my pocket, gripping my faculty ID, my thumb snapping the edge of it, then humming through the business cards.

"There you are," continued Kriel, not missing a beat. "Progress! Now we've got a price range, and forty-five grand is apparently way out of it, if I read you right."

"Way *way* out."

"How's fifteen to twenty thousand?"

"A lot more in line." Even at 20K I'd still be left with enough cash to avoid work during my leave, the inheritance from my folks making the difference between eating beans and a nice steak grilled on the fantail.

Kriel nodded, rubbed his chin whiskers, scanned the boats in stock once again. "Don't see one I'd like to sell ya out there now," he said at last. "But I think there'll be a couple vessels in that price range comin' in this week. You gonna be around?" he wondered, giving me a piercing look.

"Just for the weekend. I'm a teacher in Minneapolis," I explained. "But I'll be finished there after next week."

"And that's when you'll need the boat."

"If I can afford to leave Jens and Gert and buy from you."

"Hah!" boomed Kriel again. "Good enough."

I departed with another firm handshake and a few of Kriel's business cards, which I'd have taken anyway if he hadn't first offered them with this suggestion: "For friends of yours." A disturbing prompt since I felt hard-pressed to come up with even a half dozen names of people I would call *friends*, let alone *good* friends, people I'd proudly send to Kriel. I had let all of that slip away too when my marriage broke up. Except for Kevin.

With still a lot of Saturday afternoon sunlight to enjoy, though, I decided to refamiliarize myself with some of the resort villages along the way up the Door Peninsula—Egg Harbor, Fish Creek, Ephraim, Sister Bay, Ellison Bay, saving a visit to the "Top o' da Thumb" and a ferryboat ride over to Washington Island for another time. Jens's Door County guidebook told me that at its base the Door Peninsula is about eighteen miles wide, narrowing to around three miles at its tip. The whole county is simply one long limestone ledge and a part of what's known as the Niagara Escarpment. This extensive bank of rock arcs well beyond

Door County and runs through Canada, all the way to New York State. There it helps to create Niagara Falls. A damn impressive stretch of scenic real estate. But, as I discovered, not without its mysteries. I began to rethink the night before. Why was the news article I read so different from what I saw?

The most popular peninsula villages are on the western side of the county, all of them organized around snug valleys with gorgeous natural harbors tucked between towering tree-covered limestone cliffs—great places to evade misery and evoke mystery.

That evening, pleasantly full from a traditional Door County fish-boil dinner, I stretched out on my bed at The Wayfarer Haven, staring at the late news, wanting only an updated weather report, my optimism renewed. But when the brunette news girl, her face rigidly serious, mentioned an "internal police investigation in response to rumors surfacing since the officer's death," I sat up, tense with recognition. That troubling sound bite, however, was her full text on the matter. "Dammit," I muttered in frustration. I was exhausted. So I shut off everything and focused on one thought: With Kriel in the picture, anything and everything was possible. But the last image I saw before falling asleep was that cop car passing me on the bridge, and the cop's face, intent on pursuit.

Waking slowly Sunday morning, I knew I had to get back to Minneapolis for a change of clothes, if nothing else. I also had to grade those student essays I'd brought along but had yet to take out of the Jeep. First, though, I wanted a good breakfast and a local paper. I was anxious again to learn if any new information was available on the death of Officer Charles Parnell.

Minutes later, seated in a busy, nearby restaurant called Mom's Pantry, anticipating the imminent arrival of my "Fisherman's Special" breakfast platter, I found only one article on Parnell in the *Bulletin*—a brief obit. I did learn that he'd been a local star athlete and had attended University of Wisconsin–Green Bay himself for three years, majoring in secondary education, of all things, though he never graduated. Instead, he had left school early to pursue a career in law enforcement. I read that, like mine, his parents were both deceased. The article revealed that his only living next of kin was an older sister who lived in Texas. There was no mention in the obit of wives, ex-wives, or children.

What I *didn't* see in this article, or anywhere near the article, was any statement showing that the police department desk jockey I'd confided in had taken my information seriously. There was no boldfaced, boxed request that "the anonymous caller from last Friday evening please contact local police again for follow-up questions about what he witnessed on Tower Drive Bridge." Still, on my way out of the county, I kept the Jeep's radio tuned to the local news station. All I heard was an endless, mind-numbing string of announcements about weddings, funerals, garage sales, pet adoptions, and every *other* area car accident. Nothing more about Parnell or the information I'd offered.

So my mood on the drive back to Minneapolis for what could very well be the final days of my Hoover High teaching career was alternately upbeat and somber. Meeting

Kriel inspired limitless optimism; thinking about Parnell gave me conscience pangs.

Monday morning I managed to secure my students' fleeting respect and cooperation when I announced: "Not only do I have your essays graded, but I'm pleased to tell you they were very good company over the weekend." In truth, I'd done the bulk of the grading late Sunday night after a hard day's drive. "And now," I continued, "I'm going to spell out *exactly* what you'll need to study for our final exam." A declaration met by generous applause. It seemed as if my students were as determined not to rile me as I was to have them under control. No academic choke jobs appeared in the last week, no parents angling for better grades, no Nick Cassalatos looking to tell me off.

Nor would I have any sort of confrontation with the administrators at Hoover. My request for "Leave Without Pay" would not be denied. In fact, to the head of personnel in our school district, my somewhat tardy request was a no-brainer. She knew she could easily replace a "pricey veteran" like myself with some rookie teacher earning less than two-thirds of my princely pay. Not only would she let me go and wish me luck, she might publicly hope for my "non-return" on economic grounds.

As I made final preparations to leave one life behind, I had a last conversation with the best of that life, Kevin Vesical, who gave me an update on the worst of it—my ex, Margot.

"She pulled even with me at a stoplight in Uptown," Vesical reported.

"Oh yeah? She see you?"

"No. Because in her passenger seat, I mean *right there* next to her, riding shotgun and wearing a shoulder belt, was one of her dogs, a chocolate Lab. And she was talking to it, man. I mean, gesturing and nodding, making eye contact, having a real conversation. And the dog seemed to be *listening.* Staring back at her with rapt attention, like the two of them were—"

"On a date?" I cut in.

"*Exactly!*"

Before I could leave Minneapolis, I had to first withdraw my savings, about $5,000 over my inheritance, and clean up my apartment. The new occupant of my stagnant studio space would inherit my mattress-on-the-floor bed, a few mismatched dishes and silverware, and an aluminum lawn chair with frayed lime-green nylon webbing. I took with me a poster scene of a calm birch-ringed lake on a bright cloudless morning with a single fisherman casting from his wooden rowboat. Beneath that nostalgic image was a message: "Our life is frittered away by detail. Simplify, simplify." Amen, Henry David.

I decided to run Lake Harriet one more time, a farewell lap. Outside, the late afternoon was still balmy and bright, a terrific early June day, and as I stretched, loosened up, and began the short jog to my three-mile run around the lake, my outlook remained jaunty until I reached her house, Margot's, once our house. Since early April when I'd started running the lake again, I had never allowed myself even a glimpse at the neat, little Craftsman-style bungalow, with its "million-dollar view" of Lake Harriet. Instead, I'd actively focused my thoughts on anything but

Margot whenever I glided past the old neighborhood block. Now I wondered why I hadn't found someplace else to run. Could I secretly be thinking that she might spot me cruising by one day, call out to me, fall in love with me all over again? In our first beginning-of-the-end conversation, thirteen months earlier, her flawless face was gaunt as she announced: "I need more than teaching school can ever provide, JP. I want out of this marriage and this lifestyle."

Those words caused real pain, the same kind of pain, in fact, that I was feeling now—the same burning in my lungs and pounding in my ribcage, the same light-headedness, the same sudden disorientation, the same weak-kneed tremors in my legs, only now those afflictions resulted from pushing myself much too hard down the final stretch of my final Lake Harriet lap. So, as I awkwardly pulled back from a wind-slicing sprint, I was amused to discover that my mental replay of a failed marriage had fully occupied my attention for nearly the last three-fourths of my run.

Catching my breath, I thought: Thank God there had been no children, no dependents. Only those dogs . . . her three big *goddam* dogs. And that was a part of our life I didn't miss at all.

CHAPTER 5

After my run, I noticed a message light flashing on the phone. The call had come from Kriel in Sturgeon Bay, offering a newsy update: *"This message is for JP Griffin. Kriel here, from Bay Marina, to let you know I just got a cruiser in that could be, should be right for you. I'll hold the vessel if you can call and confirm your interest. You're not obligated or anything. Not trying to rush you or pressure you, but I got buyer lists pinned up all over the walls here. Lotsa folks lookin' for the same things about now, okay? So give me a call. Hope to hear from you soon. "*And he ended by repeating his various phone numbers—office, cell phone, answering service—three times. Now that's a salesman. I called Kriel back immediately and told him I'd be heading his way very early the next morning, would likely arrive by noon.

Departing the Twin Cities before dawn, I rolled into the Bay Marina at exactly 11:49. I parked and headed straight for Kriel's office. But he'd spotted me and come outside to greet me before I was even halfway to the building.

"A sign of authentic seriousness," he said, nodding, vigorously pumping my hand, then snapping off his wire rims to squint at me.

"What is?"

"Being on time for a sales conference, let alone a few minutes early."

"In Kriel I trust."

He laughed at that. "Let's have a look, okay? It was fifteen to eighteen thousand, right?"

"That's the range."

"Good."

He beckoned me to follow, and we walked down the shoreline until we came to a small inlet cluttered with finger piers, portable units.

"Over there," said Kriel, pointing to a smaller, white cabin cruiser, but one shaped like the Thompson I'd asked about the previous weekend.

"Uh-huh," I said noncommittally, eyeing the vessel. "Why is it so much cheaper?"

"Well, think of this one as the Chevrolet of cabin cruisers. Not all boats are created equal."

"What is it?"

"A deal!" chanted Wally Kriel, clapping his hands again. I was trying to decide if I could get to like the guy.

"I meant, what brand?"

"You're lookin' at a great starter boat and a real cream-puff in the world of pre-owned watercraft. That's a twenty-six-foot Bayliner Ciera, the popular 'Command Bridge' model, and a lot of boat for the buck. Powered by a Volvo 225, with dual control stations, upgraded GPS navigation electronics, all the bridge covers, cabin heater, sleeping for six, nice galley, stand-up head with sink, plenty of storage, bow platform with the anchor roller, and . . . you want me to go on?"

"I'd like to go aboard."

"Then let's take a look." And Kriel led the way down to the finger pier where the Bayliner was moored. "Something else you should know," Kriel continued, as he unlocked the cabin. "Since we just got this one in, as I said, we haven't done more than the superficial cleanup—washed down the exterior, checked the mechanics to make sure everything's functioning properly, checked fluid levels, picked up any clutter or garbage layin' around that got left behind, things like that. So it's not fully detailed, okay? What I'm leading to is we can knock some off the price if you want to do the detail maintenance yourself, go into it with a limited warranty."

"What's that involve, the detail maintenance?"

"I'll explain everything, give you a schedule and checklist, if that's the route you want to go. Came to us in real good shape, though."

"Fine."

"But there's one funny thing, considering your plans. Here's the only personal item sitting out we hung on to, I think. Found it right next to the pilot chair."

Kriel handed me a paperback entitled *Super Sail: Cruising Door County Waters: A Beginner's Guide* by Nelson Brite. I smiled and started paging through it. The text was unblemished by underlinings or marginal notes. But it seemed propitious—this boat seemed to want me.

"Book first came out around the time this vessel was built. Always kept a few for sale in the office, then one day it isn't in print. Author's a local who's written many books, so maybe this one'll come back. Anyway, it's still a damn useful guidebook, especially for a newcomer. So be sure and read it, *carefully*."

Nodding, holding up the book, I said, "But this only comes with the boat."

"Goes without saying," Kriel replied.

I followed his guided tour and liked what I saw. The blue and white–trimmed interior appeared lived-in, used, but not abused. The previous owners had obviously respected the vessel and maintained it fairly well. I saw no cuts or stains on the light gray upholstery, no cracks or scratches or gouges in the teak woodwork or cabinetry, no loose wires, no missing handles. I saw that a good cleaning and polishing were in order, but beyond that . . .

I commented, "It does seem nice. Who owns it?"

"Woman in Dallas, Texas, of all places. She wants it sold yesterday. Liquidating assets to meet big medical expenses, I heard."

"Uh-huh."

"So, you're interested?"

"Depends. How much?"

"The woman, Mrs. Sebring, said, 'At least eighteen.' But that's a little high, considering it's an older vessel, and there's been so little dealer prep and all. Don't know where the hell she got that figure."

"What's reasonable?" I asked.

"Gimme a number. We'll see what we can do."

"Okay." I took a deep breath. "How's fifteen?"

Wally "The Deal" Kriel let his mouth sag open theatrically, placed his big right hand over his heart, feigning total shock. "You're jokin'!"

"That's not a good number?"

"Son, I mean JP, you are lookin' at a very special vessel here, a fairly rare model, a very *popular* rare model, a very popular rare model in *really good condition*! You don't think I can do better for Mrs. Sebring than fifteen large? I haven't even tried my call-up list yet—You know, those people who say, 'Wally, if you ever get a cream-puff Bayliner Ciera call me right away, and I don't care what your price is.'"

"You're turning down fifteen."

"I could get *twenty* from a few folks I know. Tell you what—gimme sixteen-five and we'll cut the bullshit and put this deal together. And you'll be getting a whole lotta boat for your money, a boat with at least a rock-solid Kriel limited warranty, a boat you could peddle and make money on if you let it go when it still seems like summer. In addition," Kriel continued, sounding more and more like an infomercial, "you'll have a personal session with me on how to operate, navigate, and maintain the vessel. Why? Because I like you. And Mrs. Sebring will get the cash she seems to need in such a big hurry."

Obviously, I was a motivated buyer, but also a very naive and very trusting buyer, a buyer with very little money, no job, and who knows what future. Teacher pay wasn't going to support a yachting lifestyle. It couldn't even sustain a two-income marriage. Hadn't Margot given up teaching and me because of money? And hadn't she said, "Already I can't stand the thought of being stuck in a career where no matter how hard you work or how productive you are or how knowledgeable you become in your subject, you're still paid just the same as some lazy bullshitting goof-off who does virtually nothing for thirty years." Still, being desperate to find a new place to live right now, I was willing to take what she would call "irresponsible financial risks." I wanted to begin my new life immediately. And because this boat looked cozy, manageable, I went ahead and asked, "Can we take it out for a trial run?"

"Absolutely!" Kriel beamed. "Just give me a minute to tell my secretary I'll be gone." Kriel then moved fluidly up the cabin steps and across the deck, hopping lightly back onto the finger pier, carrying his considerable bulk with a smooth athleticism that surprised me. "Take a thorough look around. Be right back. I always like this part, the test drive."

I peeked in nearly all the compartments, behind closed cabinet and closet doors, and I liked how I felt being aboard. I didn't miss Margot's opinion whatsoever. I even lay down on the permanent midship berth, stretching out comfortably in what would be my bed, a big step up from a mattress on the floor.

Next, I went aft and stepped across the cockpit and leaned over the transom, searching for the boat's name. And there it was, in perfect blue block lettering against the hull's white background: *Siren Song*. I smiled at that, sensing I'd found at least part of what I'd come looking for in Door County—a place to be, a place to hide for a while, a mobile haven where I could be away from the real world and all its frustrations, a place where I could really do some serious thinking about my past, my future, my profession, my prospects.

And I liked the mythical allusions and associations the name evoked. I mean, there I was, a poor man's Odysseus, leaving the only world I knew behind me. *Unlike* Odysseus, however, I hadn't left behind a wealthy estate and a beautiful, faithful wife and loyal, brave son.

But the boat name *Siren Song* also brought some comfort since it reminded me of my father, who hardly ever left the town where I grew up. Instead, he did his far-and-wide traveling solely in his imagination. I still remember vividly how on the long days we fished together, he'd sometimes amuse himself and me out in the boat by reciting passages from Homer, usually lines having to do with seafaring and survival.

Once, for example, we were surprised by a sudden thundershower, hardly a full-blown squall, but scary enough for two guys caught out on Lake Michigan, operating an open sixteen-foot Alumacraft fishing boat with no foul weather gear. My dad used the occasion to declaim, as we rushed for shore:

> *And Poseidon spoke, and pulled the clouds together in*
> *both hands gripping*
> *The trident and staggered the seas, and let loose all the*
> *stormblasts.*
> *So sit strong all of you, to your oarlocks, and dash your*
> *oars deep . . .*

Another time, in much quieter weather, Dad got so excited while reciting Homer that he stood up in the boat, pointed an arm heavenward, then made sweeping gestures at the shoreline and open water. But he never let go of the fishing rod in his other hand and managed to hook a big northern in mid-performance.

When Kriel returned and tossed me the keys and began loosening the bow and stern lines, he surprised me by announcing, "If you like it enough to really deserve it, the boat's yours for sixteen, final offer. So, let's find out who you really are in this deal, shall we, Professor?"

And as we shoved off, Kriel taking the controls until the boat cleared the inlet and channel, I was the one feeling empowered, in charge. That was a new feeling, one I liked.

Tying up again at the marina, Kriel said, "You haven't checked into The Wayfarer, right?"

"I drove straight here."

"Good. Because I think it's important that you spend a night aboard the vessel. Lots of guys buy without ever really sampling the lifestyle of a live-aboard. They don't know what it truly feels like to be with the boat constantly."

"That would be me . . . at the low end, of course."

Kriel laughed. "You are honest," he said, patting the control panel almost affectionately.

"Likewise . . . I hope."

And Kriel chuckled again. Then he glanced at his wristwatch. "So, you got some errands to run?" he asked. "Supplies to pick up? Maybe a little sightseeing to do?"

"Actually, yes."

"Well then, here's the cabin key. I'll have you all hooked up right away. If you don't like how you feel tomorrow morning, then slide the key under the aft seat cushion when you've locked up. I'm taking off tonight, going down to Milwaukee to price some late-model used stock."

"What if I do like the way I feel in the morning?"

"Then welcome aboard! Stay on the vessel till I get back. Just don't go cruising. We've got to close the sale first. And don't worry about liability. Not only do I trust you, but both you and the boat are insured as long as you stay tied up here. Be too foggy tonight, anyway."

"Dangerous."

"Not if you know what you're doing. I meant, you couldn't see our pretty night-lit coastline."

"I was thinking about that cop who sailed off Tower Drive Bridge."

"Terrible accident." Kriel began slowly shaking his head. "Because he *did* know what he was doing. According to the papers anyway."

I reached out and shook Kriel's hand. "Thanks for all your help, the test drive and accomodations, all the effort."

Kriel bobbed his head, turned and strode away toward his office. He was a busy busy man . . . unlike me.

I spent the late afternoon hours hanging around the marina, then drove into downtown Sturgeon Bay where I ate supper at The Bayou on Third, treating myself to a plate of blackened salmon and a bowl of Cajun gumbo, a volatile combination but very tasty and satisfying.

While eating, I read from Nelson Brite's *Super Sail* guidebook: "To many travelers in this area," it began portentously,

> *Sturgeon Bay, the county seat, marks the beginning of Door County. Sturgeon Bay is a shipbuilding town of over 9,500 residents, many of whom were once employed by the area's three large shipyards. But nowadays, only two shipbuilding companies remain. Tourism is the new industry of choice and emphasis, and Sturgeon Bay has many good sights to sell. For one, the Sturgeon Bay Ship Canal cuts right through it. This channel joins Lake Michigan and Green Bay and thus makes it possible for marine traffic to reach the port of Green Bay without having to risk the journey*

through Porte des Morts—Death's Door Passage—at the top of the peninsula.

The channel also makes much of Door County an island, one connected to the mainland by just two lift bridges, the old ironwork Michigan Avenue Bridge located right in the center of town and the new freeway bridge or Bayview Bridge, which skirts the town to the southeast and arcs some fifty feet above the water.

I read on for another few pages and was greatly impressed by the clarity and vividness of Brite's writing. He had a compelling style.

Following an easy after-dinner stroll, I boarded *Siren Song*, let myself into the cabin and locked up. I'd brought back no groceries, planning to eat all my meals out.

I crawled into the midship berth, covering myself with a lightweight navy blue blanket. As I drifted off to sleep, I wondered what exactly it was that Kriel expected me to experience while spending the night on a vessel securely moored in a well-protected boat basin. There was no rocking and pitching, and the marina was remarkably quiet. With the evening air becoming cool, then crisp, I dropped off in seconds, nestled comfortably, as happy as I'd been in a long long time.

It was when I woke up in the wee hours feeling chilled to the bone, needing to close the side windows against the dank fog and find another blanket, that the quality of my night aboard changed dramatically. I slid out of bed and stumbled aft, toward the storage bin. Happily, my efforts were soon rewarded. But as I pulled a matching blanket from beneath a short stack of beach towels, I inadvertently dragged out a boxy little something that went clattering across the deck in the darkness. Fully awake now, I reached for the switch that illumined the galley.

Squinting from the sudden glare, I spotted a cassette tape in its clear plastic case lodged in the opposite corner. I stooped to retrieve it, stared at the hand-printed label markings. There was a sequence of entries beginning with "No. A-1: P/B" and ending with "No. A-6: P/F." I popped the cassette into a tape player located on the instrument dash. When I hit the Play button I heard: "Testing . . . testing." A man's voice—deep, quiet, offhand. Then a time and date were named, but the year was nearly a *decade* ago. Then the names: "Raymond Bruder . . . ahhhh . . . Kay . . . um . . . Farrow . . ." were mentioned. Very curious now, but even more chilled, I pulled the blanket across my shoulders, wrapped myself into it, and eased up the volume so as not to miss a word.

> *Q: Look, you give me the driver, and we'll see what we can do about your other problem, okay?*
>
> *A: Got no problem. Wasn't there, man.*
>
> *Q: C'mon, you imbecile, you planned it. We know that, remember? Your partner already gave that up, showed us your own shitty drawing of the layout. You signed it, for godsake.*
>
> *A: Don't prove nothin'! Wasn't there.*
>
> *Q: It doesn't matter if you were there. All your pals were, and they flipped on you already. Only detail missing is the wheel man. You wanna know the truth? You're not too good at B & E, or credit union stickups either, you really aren't.*
>
> (Long pause—)
>
> *A: I give you a name, how does that work for me?*

Q: It'll help. Shows you were trying your damndest to co-
operate, to get yourself out in front of this thing. So . . .
who was it?

A: I need somethin' specific. Assurances, you know? Like,
will I get time or not? I gotta know that.

Q: Of course you're gonna do some time. Your list of pri-
ors is pretty impressive up here in this little backwater.
But any help you give us closing the book could help
cut that time . . . substantially, I would think.

(Another long pause, stretching out uncomfort-
ably—)

A: I'm thinking, suppose I give you something real big on
some other deal, something you guys been workin' on
for fuckin' years. Would that make the time go away?

Q: What deal might you be referring to?

A: That old guy, Sloan, ten maybe eleven years ago, drove
into the lake way up the county? Drove off the North-
port Pier?

Q: You're asking me?

A: You know that deal. All you guys do. Old farmer.
Drowned supposedly, but still an open file, right?

Q: And you've got the answer, huh? Why do I think next
you're gonna offer inside dope on both the Kennedy as-
sassinations, if I don't buy this line of bullshit?

A: You think I'm lyin'?! Tell you I got something. Had it
for a while now, good long while. You'd be real inter-
ested . . .

Q: Yeah? What's on your mind?

And that fragment of a conversation ended. Tired again,
still cold, I stopped the tape and crawled back onto my
bunk. I warmed up some, but stayed sleepless as ever. I felt
I'd been eavesdropping from inside a closet—the voices

had quickly become that familiar. I got up again and shut off the galley lights. Then I slipped back into the midship berth, pulled the covers over my head, and slept restlessly.

I woke up Sunday in the gray of dawn, still thinking about the first part of the tape, wondering who made it and why—troubled by it, haunted by it. I rolled out of bed and immediately loaded the cassette into the tape player again, ready to listen to Part II. But first I wanted to make coffee and toast.

In the mini-fridge under the stovetop, of all places, I had found a small coffeemaker, several foil packets of pre-measured grounds, and a half dozen filters. I set up the little machine, added water, pushed the start switch, and . . . nothing. My first reaction was *not* to check for power by merely flipping on the galley lights, but to leave the cabin, step up on the gunwale, and look to see if my electrical line was still properly plugged in on the pier. It was. The moment I jumped back down onto the aft deck and set the boat rocking, the coffeemaker came to life. And it kept brewing only if I continued to gently rock the boat. Smiling and shaking my head in wonder, I thought: Must be the marine model Mr. Coffee. Or else there's a wire loose. Either way, I got my day-starting caffeine charge and a nice edge. Then I made dry toast from a usable half-loaf I'd found behind the coffeemaker.

Stepping over to the console, I started the tape player, then sat down with my meager breakfast. Suddenly more voices. This time the questioner was the same, but the interviewee was a woman whose voice sounded too much like Margot's. It wasn't her voice, but the tone and timbre were familiar. The conversation seemed to start in mid-sentence with:

> W: —have to get to work.
>
> M: Coffee?
>
> W: No, I don't want any coffee. I want to know why you made me come in here. You better have a damn good reason. This looks like harassment.
>
> M: Your name came up in a recent conversation. I hope you can help us with some details, clear up some discrepancies. All right so far?
>
> W: So far? You haven't said a damn thing yet, so far. I still don't know what the hell you're talking about, and in five minutes I'll be late for work.
>
> M: Then let me finish. The week before Sloan disappeared, he received at least seven phone calls from this number—Treasure Telemarketing.
>
> (Pause—)
>
> W: . . . So?
>
> M: So, the calls were made when you worked there.
>
> W: So?! You know how old I was when I worked there? I was just a kid. It was a part-time job.
>
> M: They were all made from your desk, your extension. We traced them.
>
> W: You don't have shit, do you? Anybody at that place could have made any calls to anywhere. It was a goddam boiler-room phone bank, for chrissake.

What was this? I wondered. Some cop grilling a hood and now his doxy?

Next, I heard the scraping of chair legs, the scuffling of feet, the clicking of high heels against linoleum. Then the woman said:

W: *So you're not going to arrest me for something?*
M: *Not right now.*
W: *Well, shit.*

I played the entire tape and heard more of the same—the questioner, a police detective presumably, with a guy (Raymond Bruder?) in two other conversations, the questioner with the woman (Kay Farrow?) in the rest—all of them talking in circles, nobody ever quite coming out and making a statement, nobody ever making any direct accusations, only the feeling of an indistinct threat directed by the perps at the detective, nothing substantial until the end of the last interviews when the male questioner finally asked the woman:

M: *Look, let's cut directly to it this time, okay? You know him, right? Because he says he sure as hell knows you, from way back. Says you were once his . . . piece of ass is how he put it, I think.*
W: *. . . Shit.*
(Another long pause—)
M: *Now then, you want to tell me your version of history?*

Followed by this troubling exchange with Bruder:

A: *You know a helluva lot about this.*
Q: *That's my job . . . what?*
A: *I mean, you know things nobody could know. Unless you were actually at Northport that night.*
Q: *How could I be there? I was in high school.*
A: *I bet you weren't in any high school when it happened. Was on a weekend, remember? Check it out. I know I will.*

Q: When? You're not going anywhere.

A: Goin' out the door. You got nothing on me. If you did, there'd be charges. But maybe I got something for you.

Q: Like a full confession?

A: Like a deal you can't refuse, you wanna keep your damn job.

There was no response, and the tape recorder clicked off. The cassette had run out.

And I sat on the pilot's chair, toast crumbs scattered over me, coffee gone cold, mouth agape. Then I rewound the cassette and put it back in the storage bin. And that's when it finally struck me—since the tape I'd listened to was simply a bunch of excerpts, wasn't it possible that the full-text originals were here too? So I searched all the nearby cabinets and cubbyholes but found no other cassettes.

Though tempted to do otherwise, I decided to leave the tape right where I'd found it until I could figure out what to do with the thing. Turn it over to the cops maybe? But hadn't I just risked sharing key information with the police regarding Officer Parnell? And what use had they made of that?

CHAPTER 6

With Kriel gone and my Jeep packed with all my worldly goods, I was in a sort of no-man's-land that day, homeless and anxious. I couldn't very well move aboard *Siren Song* until I legally owned it, but neither would it be smart to rent a room at The Wayfarer and continue to leave my Wrangler fully loaded. What I *could* do, I decided, was clean up and then go out for fresh supplies—enough food and drink for me to eat and sleep on board the boat for the coming night. Kriel had, after all, hooked up *Siren Song* to water and electricity, so I couldn't imagine that he wouldn't expect me to try out the galley, the minifridge, etc. And while I couldn't recall if Kriel had said when he'd be back, I couldn't decide not to buy *Siren Song* just because I'd had one sleepless night.

It was only later, when I was on the Lake Michigan side of the peninsula, hiking the White Trail leading to Cave

Point County Park, that I thought again about the cassette conversations. They were not as inspiring as the waves that relentlessly carved out deep hollows in the sheer rock before me, but just as mysterious.

At Bailey's Harbor, 10 miles away, I decided to check out the yacht club there and learn if dockage was possible on short notice. The club looked poised and prepped for a fine tourist season. Planters were full of daffodils and peonies and irises and tulips, while the club shop was well stocked with sweatshirts, caps, beach towels, swimsuits, water toys, folding lounge chairs, all labeled DOOR COUNTY in some form or fashion. And yes, they very likely would have a slip for me on fairly short notice.

I didn't get back to the Bay Marina complex till late in the afternoon, but I arrived with a genuine excitement about being aboard my own vessel. I told myself I would sleep that night. To my surprise, I found Wally Kriel standing on the finger pier next to *Siren Song*. With his hands locked behind him, feet firmly planted at shoulder width, his back ramrod straight, he looked like a naval officer inspecting a warship, his gaze drifting up and down, then back and forth, over the yacht.

When he heard my approach, he turned to face me, flashed a big smile, pulled off his wire-rims, gestured grandly at *Siren Song*, and said, "Looks good *now*, don't she? Know why?"

I shrugged, grinned tentatively.

"Had 'er *fully* detailed. Threw that in for no charge."

"Why? You said you weren't going to."

"You must be an A-list customer, huh? Besides, the cleaning crew had a little too much free time between assignments. Can't let those boys sit around, they get used to it."

So again we stepped aboard *Siren Song*, now sparkling white in the sun, the brightwork gleaming, all the wood trim aglow, the interior virtually spotless.

"Let your training begin!" chanted Kriel, clapping me on the shoulder. "Final paperwork'll be here shortly."

"What about all the things I found in the cabinets and lockers and bins?"

"All yours, if you want 'em. We're selling this one 'as is.' So if you find a treasure map or a diamond ring, it's just my tough luck. And, looking around, there seem to be some useful accessories onboard," Kriel added.

I nodded, suspicious, reluctant to mention what I'd already discovered.

But that night I thought about the tape a lot more. Who were those people talking? What crime were they discussing? Should I go to the police in person this time or, if not, confide in Wally Kriel? I decided to do neither, took two aspirin, and slept like a sack of rivets.

For the next two days, still waiting to officially close the deal on *Siren Song*, I moved aboard the cruiser and took several hours of on-site instruction from Wally Kriel. He patiently showed me how to operate and handle the vessel, how to understand the indications of the gauges and instruments and warning lights, how to read area coastal charts. Surprisingly, Kriel spent maybe one-fourth of our time together on the fundamentals of docking.

"More guys screw up themselves and their vessels by not knowing how to tie up in various conditions," he explained.

"More so than any kinda foul weather. But that's another topic," he added.

I read Nelson Brite's 150-page, photo-filled book *Super Sail* twice, underlining and boxing passages about local history, bracketing key terms like "showers available," and flagging pages that cited water depths, buoy markers, special scenery—things I'd need for future reference.

By the morning of my third day of apprenticeship, I became officially a boat owner. At that point, I'd also worked out a very tentative itinerary, having—with Kriel's help and considerable local influence—obtained dockage guarantees up and down the peninsula at marinas where "transient boats" with "live-aboards" were welcome "on a short-term basis." So I was anxious to be presented with the bill of sale. To say I was shocked on reading the name of my boat's actual previous owner would be ludicrous understatement, for *Siren Song*'s immediate past skipper had been none other than Charles J. Parnell, the Green Bay cop who had died so spectacularly when his squad car sailed off the Tower Drive Bridge and into the Fox River.

After Kriel handed over the owner's certificate, I sensed him watching me, waiting for a reaction. Before I could comment, he said a bit reluctantly, I thought, "You feel it'll bring you bad luck, we can cancel the sale. But the guy didn't have it a year. Bought it from the original owner who obviously babied it. And this Mrs. Sebring? That's Parnell's sister, but she's in tough shape, too. About gone, actually. MS, I think they said. No wonder she needs money."

"Well, I still want it. It's got to be mine," I decided. "I'll take my chances."

"So ironic," remarked Kriel, slowly shaking his head. "I think Officer Parnell had planned a summer aboard, too.

He was already living on the vessel full-time when he died. And clearly he maintained it well."

I paused, then recommitted. "Show me where to sign," I said.

Late in the morning of Day Three, the last of my initial period of instruction, with my vessel fully provisioned for a week of cruising, with my Jeep tucked safely away on a back lot of Kriel's vast marina complex—"Park it there as long as you need," Kriel had said—I was finally set to begin my own freshwater odyssey. I had placed a large portion of my remaining cash and travelers checks in a safe deposit box at a Sturgeon Bay bank and hidden the rest aboard the boat, rigging a little tilt shelf in the cabinet beneath the galley sink.

But unlike Odysseus, my quest to honor my dad's dream and maybe find my true self was a journey scheduled for just ten weeks, not ten years. And hopefully my trip wouldn't cost me the lives of any crew (I had none) or the destruction of my ship.

Before departing, I made *Siren Song* even more like home by taping up the Thoreau "Simplify, simplify" poster on the ceiling over my berth. Thus, it would always be the last thing I'd look at before falling asleep each night. I also set up my dad's old compass on the pilot-seat dash, while stowing his Gloucester fisherman's rain hat on a shelf in the pilot console. As for the brass ship's bell that my father had left me, what I did was make the short drive over to The Wayfarer Haven where I found Jens at the front desk. I held out the six-inch-diameter ship's bell and said, "Maybe you can use this for decoration or something."

Jens looked up at me, a smile beginning to form.

"It was once my dad's," I explained. "But I'd like you to have it. In appreciation for your kindness and for connecting me with Wally Kriel," I added.

I believe Jens's eyes were misting over when he said softly and slowly but firmly, "We . . . would . . . be . . . honored."

He accepted the bell, shook my hand, and said, "Good luck on your journey, son. And thank you." Holding the polished brass bell so carefully with both hands, like Margot used to hold the face of Romeo, her chocolate Lab, reverently. Why had I never imagined taking a voyage like this with her?

Because nothing I could have planned would have been enough to satisfy Margot. Like Gatsby when he first met Daisy Buchanan, I was too poor to play in the league where she thought she belonged. And by staying in teaching, I never would get rich enough to play up. So when Margot's voice became full of money, I was quickly dropped from her conversation. Margot dumped me and moved up on her own. She changed careers, met another guy with far more lucrative prospects, and secured her future. I could still recall her parting speech almost verbatim:

"I'm not who I was when me met and married, okay? And I'll never be that girl again. I'm a fighter now. I want to be someplace where I can *compete* and *win*, understand? Go for the big money, but even better—the real power. Get the rewards I've earned through my own stubborn individual effort. But you, you're exactly who you were the day we met, and you like being that person. You're not restless, you don't want to change and grow. But you've *got* to change, you've got to create a *real self* . . . or everything essential *dies!*"

In response, I quipped, "You sound like Ayn Rand in heat."

Margot was not amused.

But now look at me—restless and *so* ready to change. Happy, Margot?

My first scheduled stop was Egg Harbor, where I had a four-day mooring commitment at the municipal marina. Once there, I planned to explore the town, then cruise southwest and anchor off some of the small islands nearby. Maybe go ashore. Kriel had even tossed in an inflatable dinghy to "show good faith and motivate you to come back to me when you want to trade up," he'd said. "And sooner or later everybody wants to trade up. Repeat business, that's the *real* action."

I found myself wondering if Parnell might eventually have traded up. Or if he really had plans to follow an itinerary like mine when he was free. Maybe he'd already made the peninsula coastline tour many times. Maybe I would pull into marina after marina and be mistaken for him. With every passing hour, I became more and more obsessed by the chance nature of our connection—here I was cruising on his boat, after glimpsing him just once before his death dive.

Near the end of my first week of short test cruises and day-long fishing trips, when I had all but put the audiotape out of my mind, I was anchored securely in calm waters near uninhabited Green Island. Some ten miles southwest of Egg Harbor, the island didn't look particularly inviting. As I sprawled out on a deck chair in the sun, drink in hand, I thought about keeping a journal of my activities since I'd arrived in Door County. But while I had plenty of pens, I had no paper, no notebook.

So I decided to see if there could possibly be some paper aboard, an unused logbook, *anything* with blank pages to write on. I checked all the likely places—drawers and cabinets and cubbyholes. I tried looking in the forecabin, then the bow compartments where I pulled up the V-berth cushion that covered a matching set of ample storage bins. In one, I not only found a new, unmarked accounting ledger but also discovered another small treasure trove of useful items.

There was a far more comprehensive tool kit than the one I'd thrown together before setting off; this one even included two sets of surgical gloves for the fastidious mechanic. Also a pump-out kit, an extra window screen, and a pile of folded canvas—probably part of the bridge covers. In the other compartment, I noticed a cardboard box hidden by more canvas. Pulling the box free, I saw it was labeled USED PARTS, but inside I was thrilled to find a load of paperback novels, mysteries, nearly all of them— at least those on the top two layers—books by Floridian John D. MacDonald, his Travis McGee series.

I had heard of MacDonald but never read his books, so I picked a title at random off the top of the collection and set it aside to sample later. Looking again in the box, I lifted up another few books and saw that the first *three* layers were simply more of the same, a mother lode of MacDonald. How many McGee books were there? I wondered. Twenty? One detail I noticed immediately was that all the novel titles contained a color reference, serving as mnemonic tags, no doubt, helping JDM fans to avoid buying the same book twice.

With the sun shining brightly in another nearly cloudless mid-June sky, a cool gentle breeze stirring the air in my cozy cabin, my head and shoulders propped up against a wall of pillows, in swim trunks and a T-shirt, I forgot about my note-taking. Instead, I lay aboard my gently rocking boat, reading my first MacDonald mystery, *The Deep Blue Goodbye*. Instantly, I was hooked, pulled in, feeling at once totally connected—considering my present circumstances and setting—to a life in Fort Lauderdale, Florida, at the Bahia Mar Marina, aboard a fifty-two-foot cruisable barge-style houseboat, moored frequently at Slip F-18, amidst partyers and paramours. Travis had no wife but he did have plenty of women—compliant pleasers, feisty teasers, and ruthless anglers. Much like the old and new Margots.

As the afternoon ended, I finished one complete novel and started another. The character of McGee, a self-proclaimed "salvage expert" who makes his living by finding things that others have lost and then taking a 50 percent share of the recovered value, seemed remarkably relevant to me just now. But McGee also helped people, tried to right social wrongs. I liked the man's take on life and his outspokenness. For example, while recovering for various clients (according to the foreword) their lost jewels, lost cash, lost art, lost land, lost reputations, McGee would make offhand comments about the world being gray and sideways and all cages being frightening and guilt being the most merciless of diseases.

Among the many endorsement blurbs plastered all over the book covers was one that summed up McGee this way: "Travis is the All-American Hero of our capitalistic system: crafty, glib, well-read, forceful, self-seeking, luxury loving, handsome, huge, ambivalent, and more than a little bored with the American Dream. He isn't trying to save America, he is trying to save himself." Exactly the opposite of myself, except for the last sentence. God, if only life (my life in particular) could imitate art.

I decided to take a break and check out *Siren Song* for any immediate maintenance needs. Then I'd go for a chilly swim/bath in the shallow bay behind me, and finally get organized for my scheduled stop the next morning in Sister Bay, a jaunt of twenty-plus miles to the northeast. But MacDonald's grip on me held, so rather than doing chores, I grabbed some paper, sat down at the dinette table, and thought deeply for three minutes. Then I wrote: *Things are never so bad they can't get worse.*

MacDonald and McGee kept me awake and reading late into the night, the next installment featuring a successful attempt by McGee to avenge the murder of a former girlfriend while exposing the deathly real-estate-funding fraud perpetrated by her husband. While I waited to drift off to sleep, my mind, my imagination, was brimming with new possibilities. I was happy to have so many JDM titles yet to read. I was thankful that Officer Parnell had saved MacDonald's work for me to discover. Then, at the edge of sleep, I remembered that mysterious cassette tape I'd found my very first night aboard *Siren Song*. I would pull it out tomorrow, maybe have another listen, maybe hear something different and begin to understand. Mystery was fast becoming my *metier*.

But I decided not to wait till morning. I chose instead to get up and retrieve the cassette again. And that's when I discovered it was gone. I stood staring down at the storage cabinet where I'd left it, wondering, naturally, who could have taken it and why. My only candidates for the part of petty thief were Wally Kriel and some member of his detailing crew. So what was I supposed to do now? Complain to Kriel? Call in the detail boys and confront them one by one? Maybe provoke a scene that would create for me everything I was so conscientiously trying to avoid—functionless anxiety, troublesome involvements, compromised anonymity? I had come here just to be alone, to sort out my feelings about teaching, parents, personal relationships. I didn't want to get into anything with anybody. Besides, it wasn't really my tape in the first place. And since I had no clue as to what it was supposed to be or mean, why should I care who took it now? I shrugged and dismissed the whole situation. Somewhat less at ease, I still managed to sleep fairly well.

The next morning I overslept, but I decided to stick with *The Plan* and make my scheduled run up to Sister Bay where I had a slip waiting at the expansive village marina. I wanted to sample the sights there, shop in what was said to be the best bookstore in the county: Pastimes Books, a family-owned, independent, non-chain, non-mall, non-blockbuster-hyping enterprise. The store supposedly housed the most comprehensive list of titles by Door County writers, about Door County subjects. But first, purposely starved, I wanted a late morning breakfast/lunch at perhaps the area's premier landmark: Al Johnson's

Swedish Restaurant, with its imported notched logs and sod roof and legendary food.

By the time I had tied up, checked in at the dock office, and walked the short distance to Al Johnson's, the surge of early risers and eaters was letting up slightly. I stepped into the lobby, approached the "Please wait to be seated" sign, and was immediately attended to by a pretty waitress in full Swedish folk costume who asked if I wanted to be seated (I nodded) and if I was a "party of one" (I nodded again, embarrassed). Then she glanced across the dining room and set off with me in tow. As we made our way through the lingering crowd, sidestepping high chairs and shopping bags and camera equipment cases, I noticed a vocal group of eight or nine middle-aged men, all seated at a large round table in a far corner of the restaurant. With their shaggy hair and beards, plaid shirts and rolled-up sleeves, well-worn jeans and scruffy work boots, they could have been anybody local, any area native—a commercial fisherman or charter boat captain or construction worker. They certainly didn't resemble the bulk of the restaurant's other patrons—the day-tripper tourists and condo-owning summer people, in their bright Bermudas and dark glasses.

I stared over, noticing that above the general din I could hear them talking heatedly one second, with much gesticulating and finger pointing, then bursting into uproarious laughter a moment later. The waitress had stopped too.

"Sir?" she inquired.

Turning back to face her, I smiled and said, "The Rotary Club?" Nodding at the round table.

She gave me a quick laugh, rolling her eyes. "Hardly. See the guy with the droopy handlebar mustache?"

"Sure."

"Well, that's Nelson Brite, our very own local celebrity author. Our local one-man literary industry actually— writer, publisher, talk show host, performance artist, painter, you name it. Some book reviewer in Chicago or New York once called him 'America's best *under*appreci- ated writer.'"

And of course I remembered the guidebook, *Super Sail,* a helluva good read all around. So I sneaked another look at Brite. He wasn't a big man, but he was clearly in charge—making wisecracks, mediating conflicts, motion- ing for attention. He looked like a first-rate raconteur in the great Mark Twain tradition.

"Who're the others?" I asked.

"The Group. They're all local artists of one kind or an- other—painters, potters, poets—the whole alliterative bunch. They've been meeting here now and then for years. Nelson is a regular, though. Almost every day."

The waitress's quipping caught my interest, compelled me to take a better look at her. She appeared to be straight out of central typecasting—the Classic Nordic— her cute, close-fitting, embroidered Swedish dress, her clogs, a bright clear face with just a hint of makeup and marred only by a thin but obvious little scar high on her left cheekbone. Blonde hair thick and shining, falling gracefully to her shoulders, her body trim and strong, a *young* woman, perhaps in her late twenties at most, a few years my junior, maybe twenty-eight to my thirty-two. She grinned as she caught me studying her blue eyes, and I smiled back. Then she pointed to a table by the window, saying, "Is this okay? You need a view."

Was this another instance of "meeting cute," as screenwriters put it? Because already this girl was reminding me of Margot, though they didn't look anything alike. When I first met Margot on her first day at Hoover, she had said, "I've heard you're really good, and that I should talk you into being my faculty mentor ASAP."

Stunned by Margot's dark sultry looks and effortless charm and intoxicating self-confidence, I said, "Consider my files *open.*"

"Because I'm really nervous about this," she added, winking and pulling aside a spill of glossy black hair.

"Relax," I had said. "You've now got a friend in the business."

"Sir?" the waitress prompted.

And I refocused, looked around, then realized I couldn't have gotten a better table for my *party of one,* even if I'd fallen on my knees and begged the waitress for it. I could see *the world* from this table—the crowds of happy tourists passing by outside, the animated chatter of the diners around me, the hale chorus of *oooohh*s and *aaaahhhhhhh*s and guffaws coming from the Artists of the Round Table. I beamed back to the pretty waitress my best boyish grin and said, "Thanks. Couldn't be better." And seated myself, accepting the menu she handed me. Then I quickly added, "Don't go, okay? I mean, I'll order right now."

"Very well," she answered, taking out her pad and pen.

I scanned the many options.

"Have you eaten here before?"

"A few times, years and years ago. I was only a kid."

"So you don't need any advice on selections."

"I don't know. Maybe. What's included with this one?"

The waitress stepped a little behind me to look over my shoulder at the open menu. Quite by chance, I think, she placed her hand gently on the top of my other shoulder.

Her small gesture sent an electric rush right through me, and my mind filled with tragic words and images from some newsmagazine TV show I'd seen months back, a segment where a number of smart, professional, retired widows and widowers, divorcees and "separateds" explained how much they missed the little intimacies, the most superficial kinds of human physical contact. With no spouses and with children and grandchildren "spread out all over the whole damn country," they admitted that sometimes they'd go to a supermarket or shopping mall just to run into some stranger "by accident." Literally walk right into someone, simply to be able to reach out and touch another person while pretending to regain their balance, which they probably were doing in the most desperate and basic sense of the word.

And again, Margot came back to haunt me, the early Margot—the affectionate, fun-loving Margot. The Margot who sneaked out of school during her prep hour and surprised me by bringing back a Caribou Cooler, still cold, and a fresh cinnamon roll, still warm. The Margot who cheered me on at the faculty/student basketball game, a scholarship fund-raiser, hollering encouragements like "Take it to 'im, skywalker! You da *man*!!" Whether I had the ball or not. The Margot who chaperoned prom with me one spring and convinced the other young faculty couples on duty to stay up all night, then go waterskiing at a nearby lake the next morning in full formal attire.

"Sir?" the waitress prodded. "Have you decided?"

"Oh . . . yes," I answered, stumbling, rushed back from my thoughts. Her hand left my shoulder. "This sounds good," I said, pointing to a "Hearty Special," a combination that featured eggs, sausage, and the famous Swedish pancakes responsible for the restaurant's reputation.

Looking down at me, the waitress smiled again, and I noticed her name tag. Did it say "Sigrid"? I couldn't tell for sure, and before I could sneak a closer look she walked off.

On her way to the kitchen, someone from the Artist Group called to her. It was Nelson Brite himself, who made some quick comment that got her attention, brought a look of serious concentration to her face. Another remark from Brite, though, caused her to suddenly toss her head in laughter. She followed that little outburst with a glance over her shoulder at me. I stared back, trying my best to project amused, relaxed interest.

When she returned to my table a few minutes later, carrying the perfectly prepared breakfast, I attempted, subtly I imagined, to glance again at her name tag.

"It's not my real name," she whispered.

"*Sigrid.*" I read it out loud. "So, if that's not it, what—"

"Another time," she said, hurrying away.

I was left staring down at my breakfast.

Sigrid and I said no more to each other after that because another waitress delivered the bill. So I ate my breakfast in silence and self-conscious isolation. Not too many other single diners at tables in Al Johnson's. Still, I left a generous tip and planned to stop in again in the next few days to see if I could put a real name with the gentlest touch I'd felt in months.

Later that afternoon, I returned to the village dock. Earlier, while browsing at Pastimes Books, housed in a small, plain, metal-sided one-story building on the coastal edge of Bay Shore Drive, just where the roadway rises to climb the high bluff bordering the south end of the village, I discovered that Nelson Brite was a very prolific local writer. Nearly twenty published books and I had only read one. I was impressed, so much so that I purchased three Brite titles: a collection of essays and interviews, a book of short stories, and a novel.

Now, as I entered the marina and started toward my slip, the dockmaster stepped out of his office and greeted me with "Mr. Griffin? Message for you." The man held up a small slip of paper.

"Kriel in Sturgeon Bay," the dockmaster continued. "Wants you to give him a call ASAP. Here's his cell phone number."

"Thanks," I said, accepting the note. "Where's the nearest phone?"

"No cell with you?"

"Call me *Luddite.*"

He snickered. "Use ours, if you like," he said. Then added, "Pay phone up the street and down a ways there." Pointing.

I opted for the office phone and dialed Kriel's number.

Kriel answered after only two rings with his stock phone greeting of "Yeah." I'd heard him respond that way many times during my days of apprenticeship instruction with the master salesman/yachtsman.

"Wally Kriel?" I asked ritually.

"Oh yeah. Who's this?"

"Griffin, returning your call?"

"Yeah, yeah. Got a little package here for you."

"A package?" Who would be sending mail to me in Door County?

"More like a padded envelope. Addressed to 'JP at Bay Marina.' But our address is written over another one, like it's been forwarded."

"Can you see the original address?"

"Can't read it because they put some self-sticking label over it and wrote our address on that."

I fell silent, unable to imagine who could mail me a package up here. Maybe it was Vesical, sending a farewell two-dollar plaque courtesy of Hoover High.

"You are 'JP,' right?" Kriel continued. "That wasn't some alias you laid on me," he added.

"I'm JP," I confirmed. Then, "You want me to come down and get it?"

"Actually, I have to be up your way tomorrow morning, but very early. You staying at least another night there?"

"More than that, I hope."

"Good. I'll drop it off first thing. If you look all closed up, I'll just leave it right next to your cabin door."

"Great. Thanks. By the way, Wally, do you trust your detailers?"

"Um . . . why?" Sounding careful.

"Well, a tape of mine is missing."

"I bet it fell behind something when you were rollin' 'cross the waves." Then changing the subject rapidly, "You like the boat?"

"Runs great."

"Another satisfied customer."

"Another good *deal*," I added, thinking of all the bonus equipment I'd discovered aboard. But I went to bed troubled. I knew exactly where I'd put the cassette tape, so Kriel either didn't care that I couldn't find it or he was clumsily covering for his detailers. But Wally wasn't clumsy. And what about that package?

CHAPTER 7

Waking from another restless sleep, I discovered the sun already high in the sky. I planned to eat breakfast on board, feeling raw-nerved and grainy-eyed. I sat on the edge of my berth and dragged a thumbnail across my morning stubble, thinking: Why can't I just relax and be comfortable on this boat?

But I wasn't so distressed and disoriented that I forgot Wally Kriel's promise to deliver a package. I unlocked the cabin door and peeked out. There, just as Kriel said it would be, was a 6 × 9–inch padded envelope, well secured with tape, and addressed to "JP c/o Bay Marina, Sturgeon Bay, WI." As I picked up the parcel and brought it inside to the dinette table, I wondered why Wally didn't try rousing me. Then I took out my coffeemaker and started the boat rocking. While the coffee brewed, I went to wash my face.

Moments later, with burbling coffee for background music, I sat in the dinette booth and, using a dull steak knife, carefully slit open the heavily taped little envelope.

Inside I found some pages torn from a spiral notebook and folded tightly. Opening the pages, I saw they were a letter. Along with the pages came a cassette tape, *another* cassette tape. Once again I scanned the self-sticking address label covering the original destination of the package, and when I tried oh-so-gently to peel back the label, it began to tear away the surface layer of the paper beneath. Then I noted the original cancellation stamp: FL.

I picked up the cassette identified simply as "No. B-1" and reached for the small battery-operated boom box I'd brought along to supply high-seas/open-air entertainment. Slipping in the cassette, I hit Play and heard: "Testing . . . testing . . . Raymond Bruder . . . ahhhh . . . Kay . . . um . . . Farrow . . ."

I snapped off the machine, knowing exactly what I had—a duplicate of the mystery tape I'd already listened to in full, the one that mysteriously disappeared. I glanced at the folded notebook pages and decided to read the letter. It began:

> *Dear Jimmy,*
>
> *I got the cassette tape today and I tried to listen to it but I just couldn't finish. What are you trying to tell me? Why did you send that now? Do you have any idea what's happening to me <u>right now</u>?! I find myself thinking about you (us) every day lately—every single day. I keep asking myself WHY? I keep wondering—Is that where all this started? Because of what we did?*
>
> *If we would have kept it, Jimmy, we might have been okay. People do make a life in those circumstances. But after you stopped talking to me, I was so scared and so lonely. Just like I am now, telling everything to dead paper.*

Just then the coffeemaker quit bubbling and dripping and started sparking. I jumped up to pull the plug, but my lurching rocked the boat hard enough to end the electric sizzle as well as the brew cycle. I stood over the quiet machine, smelling the acrid air, shaking my head. Still, I poured myself a steaming mug and promised to look for the loose connection, the crossed wires causing the trouble.

I took my coffee back to the dinette table and continued reading:

> *After we got back together I kept hoping that everything would be good and clear between us. But of course I didn't know that it was already too late. Did you even know I married Brad W after you disappeared? I was pregnant again, and we wandered around the country for ten years, moving from Navy base to Navy base, ending up here in Pensacola. I miscarried twice. One day Brad picked up some whore when he was drunk and ran off the road and died. And now, Jimmy, I've got ovarian cancer. God, do I wish this shit would just go away!!*
>
> *Jimmy, I hope things are going better for you than they are for me, but to tell you the truth I can't listen to that tape, ever. I'm dying, Jimmy, and nothing's going to change that. But you know what? I never told.*
>
> *So when the tape comes back to you, please don't think I don't care. You took my heart long ago. Jimmy, you have everything to live for, and you never have to be afraid anymore. Because Jimmy, I never told anyone!*
> *With Lasting Love,*
> *EC*
> *P.S. What is Slip C-45?*
> *P.S.S. Pray for me. Okay Jimmy?*

Tragedies upon tragedies here, I thought. The poor girl. But who the hell is "Jimmy"? Was slip C-45 the one *Siren Song* had occupied at Kriel's marina? I snapped on the boom box again and began scrupulous note-taking, first on the backup cassette, then the letter.

When I'd finished making a detailed record, I needed to unwind. I changed quickly to my running gear, locked up the boat, and jogged off, following the highway as it curved inland and then rose dramatically, becoming yet another challenge I had to confront.

That evening, sitting on deck in a canvas chair, sipping a beer, I let my mind continue to race. As I watched the sun set and felt the air go from pleasantly crisp to downright chilly, I tried to figure out what the taped voices possibly meant. How did the tape relate to the letter I had received? Soon I was shivering, the cold of the night air and my own fears sending me inside for a jacket or blanket.

I headed for the V-berth storage area, certain I'd seen a thick sand-colored wool poncho folded and tucked in the starboard side compartment. Holding up the V-berth cushion with one hand and gripping a flashlight with the other, I scanned the contents of the open chamber. And there was the poncho, just where I'd remembered seeing it.

I placed the flashlight beam on the cloak and reached for it. But as I pulled it out, I discovered that beneath it was a small black carrying case of some kind. Pushing the garment behind me, I leaned further into the storage space to retrieve the black case. It was an awkward maneuver. The case was buried deep and surprisingly heavy for its size.

Once I'd backed out of the V-berth completely, leaving the poncho for the time being on my bunk, I carried the black case to the dinette table and set it down carefully, shoving aside the cassette tape and letter. I thought I knew what it was, but I couldn't be sure until I'd popped the snap locks bracketing the handle and lifted the top half of the case away. Inside was an old but remarkably clean Smith Corona manual typewriter, "The Sterling" model, apparently fully functional. It looked like a machine from the 1920s or '30s. I searched for some blank paper and finally came up with a few 8 ½ × 11–inch sheets after completely emptying the chart drawer.

Next, I slid the paper into the carriage, rotated the platen, and tried the keys. They worked beautifully, perfectly, the letters printing out straight, clean, dark, and true. At least on my first five words. The ribbon must have been recently changed. *What a find!* So I decided then and there that I would do my summer journaling using this anachronistic technology, a totally personal and private way of writing that was seemingly invulnerable to the violations and invasions of computer-created and "saved" texts. I'd been schooled in computer use, of course, but my computer literacy is illiteracy when compared with that of almost any semi-bright eight-year-old. It was hard to keep up. And with computers nowadays it didn't seem to matter that "files" were "closed" or "secure" or "locked" because apparently any precocious hacker anywhere in the world could "access" them. Personal privacy has become a bigger and bigger deal for me. And for lots of other people.

So I sat up straight and tried to get something going on the machine, attempting to get used to the response of the keys, their touch, by practicing right away. I started to type the impressions generated by my receiving the puzzling letter and the duplicate tape. I tried to sort out all the "facts" I'd gathered, and quickly I filled every one of my found pages.

The Facts, as I understood them:

1. I assume that the cop doing the interviews on the tape was Officer Parnell. The tape was on his boat, in his possession.

2. The tape itself is ten years old, if the date on the label is accurate.

3. The man being interviewed—Raymond Bruder?— seemed to be a local petty criminal that Parnell was trying to connect with a break-in, perhaps a robbery.

4. But when Parnell finally had Bruder cornered, the suspect offered the cop information about an "old guy" who "drove into the lake" some "ten, maybe eleven years ago."

5. When pressed for information about that open case, Bruder implicated a woman—Kay Farrow?—who could have been the female talking with Parnell in the later conversations.

6. When confronted by Parnell with Bruder's information, Farrow became irritated and defensive but not . . . *morally outraged*, let's say, at Parnell's line of questioning. And when she asked, "So you're not going to arrest me for something?" she might be saying that there's maybe something worth arresting her for.

7. In the final exchange, Bruder seems to be going on the attack, implying that the cop/detective is himself involved in the crime.

Then the surprise appearance at my cabin door of the backup copy of Parnell's tape truly confused matters. Who was "EC"? And who was the "JP" named on the new address label, if not me? And who the hell was "Jimmy"?

Parnell's name was *Charles*, according to the newspaper and all the legal forms conveying ownership of *Siren Song* to me via Parnell's sister in Texas, Mrs. Gina Sebring.

I decided next to conceal the notes I'd just typed up and to retape the package with the cassette and letter, maybe turn them back over to Kriel and see what he did next with them. Would I dare confide to him that I'd listened to the tape? Should I risk sharing the information and implications I thought I'd uncovered? But hadn't he known all along that my boat was Parnell's? Was he directly involved in some way with this mystery? I sat paralyzed, so I decided to stall.

As I picked up my typescript, though, I realized how much I enjoyed this way of writing, composing. I liked to feel myself making actual impressions, making my words and sentences and paragraphs real one felt letter at a time, making a story—a sensible narrative—out of what I thought I knew. I liked feeling the imprinted typescript once the sheet was full, the Braille-like individuality of each line and page.

Soon I was reimagining myself as a MacDonald/Travis McGee protégé, only instead of following a ghost around in the pages of books, I would seek my own truth under open sky, amidst big water, and I would put the truth of my life in order on typed pages—one hand-driven letter at a time—using this demanding, time-consuming machine.

But that night the open skies I'd relished all day became filled with boisterous, swollen rain clouds. I closed the hatches and windows before the first big gusts of storm wind began to rake the bay and rock the hull, stretching tight the holding lines. I was happy to be in port, well laced into my U-shaped slip, in a well-protected harbor at a substantial municipal dock. It was a howling all-night rain.

The following morning all was new again. The storm had passed entirely, and the rising sun shone brightly through the freshly washed air. I had risen at dawn to begin writing, tapping out a vignette or two about my recent experiences, using my latest providential gift—the antique typewriter—and a few sheets I'd torn from the account book I'd uncovered. I quickly realized I'd have to go to town soon for some genuine typing paper.

Then hunger pangs flared and I began contemplating Al Johnson's, a good breakfast, and the chance to talk to the waitress with a name tag but no identity . . . *yet.*

CHAPTER 8

"You're back," said Sigrid, appearing next to me out of nowhere.

Surprised, I managed, "Well . . ."

"The food?" she asked, taking a menu from the rack.

"The ambience, really."

"That we can always deliver." Turning, calling over her shoulder, she said, "Follow me, please."

I was glad to obey.

And she led me once more into the crammed restaurant. As I worked my way through the clusters of diners, I felt eyes upon me. Glancing around, I spotted the writer Nelson Brite sitting alone at the lunch counter, holding up a folded newspaper, sipping coffee, tracking my progress with a bemused gaze. Another waitress, leaning toward Brite on her elbows and chatting animatedly, didn't seem to notice that she'd momentarily lost Brite's undivided attention.

Brite acknowledged my sidelong glimpse by lifting the corner of his mouth, twitching his droopy mustache, giving me a quick nod of recognition. Then, abruptly, he shifted his focus back to his own pretty waitress and his morning paper.

"How's this?" Sigrid inquired.

I looked down at the table, discovered it was exactly the same window view I'd enjoyed the other day and wondered: Was this simply a matter of good timing? Providence? Someone's Master Plan?

At that instant I decided to risk asking the waitress, "Would you mind answering a couple of questions for me?"

"Sure . . . I guess." Biting her lower lip.

"I mean, you'll tell the truth, right?"

"Depends." Looking even more anxious.

"The truth *depends*? Where's your trust?"

"Do I know you?"

"The thing is, I'm getting the feeling people here do know me, or know something about me, even though I haven't been up this way in years."

"Easily explained. You bought a boat."

"Lots of people buy boats."

"But you bought a very particular boat."

"How do you know about that?"

"Nelson Brite told me. He knows almost everything going on around here, and everybody who makes anything happen. Wally Kriel is one of his pals."

"Why does Wally Kriel or Nelson Brite or anybody else care if I bought a boat?"

"*Siren Song*. It belonged to a certain Green Bay cop, another acquaintance of Brite's."

I scanned her face. We were both still standing next to the table, but she wasn't smiling now. So, unsure of where to take the conversation, I asked, "Brite cares about boat sales?"

"Not usually. Just this one, I think."

"Why?"

"Because I named it."

"*My* boat?!"

And then the hostess, over in the restaurant lobby, raised her right arm, calling Sigrid to come back and seat the next party, a young family of five.

Before she could get away, I asked, "How'd you happen to name it?"

She gave me a parting glance, serious, frowning. "I was once married to that cop, the one who just died."

"Parnell?!"

"Uh-huh. He asked me to pick out a name, have one ready, and I chose *Siren Song*. Play on words, him being a cop."

"Really." This coincidence had all kinds of possibilities.

"I'm not a widow or anything. We were divorced a long time ago. What was the other question?" Turning toward the lobby.

"Can I see you when your shift is over?"

"Sure." Finally, Sigrid showed me a trace of a smile. "I'll be done by four today," she said, hurrying off.

Soon a different waitress, Lisa, also gorgeous, took my order and brought me my breakfast. While I downed another plate of Swedish pancakes and sausage links, I noticed Brite leaving the counter. I watched him as he worked the floor—shaking hands, patting shoulders, nodding hellos—catching a final glimpse of the writer near the entrance in a huggy exchange with Sigrid.

Just past 4:00 p.m. I stood waiting across main street, Bay Shore Drive, leaning against a storefront, watching the doors of the restaurant. Again, uneasy feelings had begun to haunt me. What was I doing even thinking of getting involved with another woman so soon after what I'd been through? And the two women—Margot and Sigrid—so unalike. One with mad ambitions, the other a waitress. Even their physical appearances were opposed: Margot— tall, thin, raven-haired, olive-skinned, sharp-edged, provocatively aloof, and Sigrid—blonde, toned, tawny, bright-eyed, sensual, excitingly warm. The very reason I'd come here in the first place was to live life unencumbered, without entanglements, without complications.

Knowing I could simply get aboard my boat, no matter who had named it, and cast off and sail away and never come back here, if that was what I really wanted to do, I had to choose. And what I decided was that, more than anything else just now, I wanted to have a nice talk with a pretty and engaging young woman. Who possessed a marvelous touch. And who might have a few good ideas about why Parnell would hang on to a decade-old tape. Who might even know a full name for "Jimmy." But how direct could I dare be with her?

At last she emerged, coming out of the restaurant, unpinning her name tag. She scanned the area, looking up and down the street, then finally across it where her gaze met mine. She waved. I waved back and started to come toward her. She got to me first.

"I always like to go down by the shore right after work," she explained as she stepped past me. "I need to look at the water, the sky, the sun." She tilted her head, inviting me to follow.

"I can see why. Another great day," I said.

So we wandered through the small park across from Al Johnson's, angling toward a narrow strip of public beach. We stood silently, surveying the harbor, watching a pair of seagulls teeter on the wind before making their point-blank dives into the bay. I spotted my cabin cruiser.

"There she is," I announced, pointing.

Sigrid followed my outstretched arm. "There *who* is?"

"The boat. *Siren Song*."

"Which one is it exactly?"

"You can't tell?"

"I've never seen it. He bought it long after we'd split up. When Nelson told me its name . . . naturally I was curious."

"Speaking of names, what's yours? I mean, your real, authentic, legal name?"

"Kelly Shelberg." She extended her hand, like a realtor meeting a client for a house tour.

I took her hand in mine and said in return, "I'm JP Griffin." Feeling the current.

"What's the *JP* stand for?" she asked, gently withdrawing her hand.

"Jason Phoenix."

She slowly let herself smile, amused, I guess. "What'd they call you in high school? Phenom? Nixo? Jase?"

"Just JP."

"Whose idea, *Phoenix*?" Serious now.

"Dad. He was a world history teacher in this little town where I grew up. Loved the ancients. Some days he'd stare out across Lake Michigan when we were fishing and recite Homer's *Odyssey*, his favorite parts."

"*Was* a teacher?"

"He's dead."

"I'm sorry."

I shrugged, feigning nonchalance.

"*Griffin*," she continued thoughtfully. Then recited: "*Griffin*—a mythical beast with the head, chest, and wings of an eagle and the torso, hind legs, and tail of a lion."

"There you go."

"And Griffin, the *ex*-teacher," she added.

And I was surprised once more. "Brite?"

"Via Kriel, I think. Who, by the way, says you're a pretty good guy."

What have I gotten myself into here? I thought. Everybody knows about me, while I know next to nothing.

Squeals of delight coming from a group of little kids playing along the beach distracted us momentarily. We watched them douse each other with plastic pails of chilly bay water.

"Nelson mentioned your job because it's something else we have in common," Kelly said.

"Teaching?"

"Leaving teaching. At least taking a break from it. Twenty days ago . . . no, twenty-*one* days ago, I walked."

"Where were you working?"

"A very nice suburb near Milwaukee."

"What subject?"

"English. Sophomore American Lit, some Basic Comp 9."

I nodded, thinking: We're way beyond coincidence now. "Kindred spirits," I said. "Nine years of American Lit sophomores." Pointing to myself.

She considered that fact a moment before replying, "Well, we either have a helluva lot to talk about, or else absolutely nothing more to say that's going to be news."

"Ahhhhh, teaching. Why did you leave?" I wondered.

The screaming beach kids were getting louder, more numerous, more distracting, more annoying.

"When I started," Kelly said, "I thought I would stay in it forever. But these last few years . . . all that functionless paperwork, the endless checklists, the bogus accountability schemes, all of it created by people who either failed miserably in the classroom or who never even set foot in an actual class of forty students. I couldn't take it anymore."

"Just like Hoover High in Minneapolis."

She placed her hand on my bare forearm. "Let's not talk shop, okay? It depresses the hell out of me."

Again her touch sent a bewildering jolt through me. Either she was 1) the sexiest woman alive, or 2) supercharged with some weird cosmic aura, or 3) I was pathetically overdue for some close human contact, something Margot denied me, once she decided to go.

"You want to see the boat?" I asked. "The complete guided tour?" Anxious now to distance myself from the noisy children.

"Permission to come aboard, sir?" she kidded.

We cut over to the village dock and strolled out to the slip where *Siren Song* was tethered.

After I'd unlocked the cabin and slid open the windows to circulate some fresh air, I asked, "Look like you thought it would?"

Kelly glanced around the cabin, scanned the bow through the windshield. "It's roomier than it looks."

"So make yourself comfortable." I gestured at the dinette and she sat down, her gaze continuing to drift about the cabin.

"Something to drink?"

"I'll have what you're having." She looked back at me, showed a quick smile.

I pulled two margarita coolers from a four-pack and mightily twisted off the tops. "Here," I said, handing Kelly her bottle. "Glass?"

"I'll rough it," she answered, holding her bottle toward me for a toast.

"Then cheers." I clinked my bottle with Kelly Shelberg's. We both took toasting sips.

Then I began, "How'd you meet him . . . Parnell? Or don't you want to talk about that either?"

"I'm okay there," she said. "And it was the same way I met you." She took another swallow from her cooler.

"He walked into the restaurant?"

"Way back during my first summer out of college. I'd just signed my first teaching contract. Green Bay."

"He must have been older than you, Parnell."

"Some, yeah."

I wanted to tell her why I was so curious, tell her about my suspected chance meeting with her ex that foggy night on the Tower Drive Bridge. Work in some questions about the tape and *Jimmy*. But I didn't, couldn't just yet. I didn't know her at all. Instead I tried, "What'd you do, fall for the uniform?"

"Uh-uh. He wasn't in uniform . . . *ever*. At least not when we dated. I didn't even know he was a cop the first two weeks, if you can believe it." She went back to her cooler for two more slow sips.

The day was mellowing nicely. The typical Door County–postcard western horizon of puffy white clouds hanging along a line of light blue sky and dark blue water had formed itself perfectly again.

Staring out at the late afternoon weather, she stated, "I *am* okay," with a little self-affirming nod.

I asked, "What'd you think he did? For a living, I mean."

"I assumed at first he was some kind of administrator, like for the Park and Rec Department. He liked working with kids, coaching, stuff like that. He said once upon a time he wanted to be a teacher, too."

"Mystery man," I commented before taking a long pull of my cooler. "Did that bother you?"

"I kind of liked it, the not knowing, at first anyway." She went on, "He didn't come into Al's like so many other guys and start by telling me how cool or connected or clever he was, or how important because of his job or money or things. He simply said he'd like to have dinner with me some evening, and I said okay.

"It wasn't until after we were married I realized that *mystery* was all I'd ever get. I mean, at first he was away a lot of the time, working or preparing for work. But then it was like he was away all the time, even when he was right next to me at home. He wouldn't open up, even to me."

"Probably made him a good cop."

"Maybe. But . . . I woke up one day and realized I didn't know the first thing about him, personally or as a police officer. And I never would. He was a guy with secrets—lots of them, I'm afraid. A haunted guy who couldn't share." Her eyes left mine and her gaze followed the view from the pilot's seat. She stared blankly until a horn blast from an incoming sloop made her flinch.

I asked, "How long were you married?"

"Not even two years," she said. "But that was almost five years ago."

"And you never heard from him again, after the divorce?"

"That's another strange thing—three, maybe four months ago I got a letter from him, the only letter he ever wrote me. And in it he said he thought he was getting closer to finding a way to deal with the behavior that caused problems for us. That's about how specific he was.

I wrote back to be encouraging. I never heard from him after that."

An uneasy silence developed. She downed the last of her cooler, handing me the empty bottle. Then she thought to ask, "What about you? Married?"

"Yeah. And also divorced."

"Same old reasons?"

"Not really. She wanted to get rich and I didn't or couldn't or wouldn't, and that bothered her a lot. She basically thought I wasn't competitive enough. Plus I didn't like her dogs. That bothered her even more."

"Oh, those controlling women," said Kelly with a wink.

"I suppose."

Kelly sighed, stared knowingly at me. "It's funny how we fellow teachers can talk, huh? Like combat vets."

"Good analogy," I judged.

"So, what is there to talk about now?" She caught my gaze, held her eyes on mine. "Hungry?" she asked.

"Real hungry."

"Let's get out of this town, then. I need a change of beautiful scenery once in a while."

"It's your car."

"Let me go back to my place and change. I'll be by for you in less than an hour."

"Okay. But you don't have to change. You look fine the way you are, very ethnic and local."

Kelly Shelberg stared down at her Al Johnson's outfit and said, "I'm dressed to yodel."

Kelly was a woman of her word, I was glad to find out. Just five minutes short of an hour she aimed a black, rust-spotted Honda Civic into the harbor parking lot, got out, and started walking down the dock toward *Siren Song*. Punctuality, I thought, watching her approach. She simply had to have been a teacher. I pushed myself up from a deck chair, checked the cabin door to make sure it was locked, and climbed onto the finger pier, setting off to intercept her. She spoke first, asking, "Is there any place special you want to try, being a tourist and all?"

"I'm hoping you have a can't-miss recommendation."

"I've got just the place."

So we shared a sort of teens-on-a-first-date-in-Door County burger-fries-chocolate malt supper at Wilson's— "Serving you since 1906"—an ice-cream shop/restaurant with its trademark red and white striped awning, located in Ephraim, the next village southwest of Sister Bay and the most picturesque of the bayside towns. Afterwards, we tried walking off our indulgent meals by hiking the shoreline, continuing southwest, passing all sorts of commercial establishments until we reached some beautiful 1920s beach cottages—several of which had been lavishly updated by folks who creatively exploited two key real estate concepts: *Grandfathered* and *Variance*.

It had been a golden afternoon and evening, and I sincerely liked Kelly. I could easily imagine teaching with her, sensing what a lively, funny, and enjoyable colleague she would be, no doubt had been for many. And I couldn't help wondering, would I have fallen for Kelly at school the way I did Margot? Or was Kelly simply a summer girl?

CHAPTER 9

Kelly drove me back to the Sister Bay dock. She surprised me with an enthusiastic kiss in the car. When I asked if she'd like to come aboard for a nightcap, she politely declined but gave me another kiss and explained that she had to rise early and be a cheerful waitress in six hours. I climbed out of her car, watched her roll out onto Bay Shore Drive and disappear into the darkness. I then walked down to my boat, a tragically empty vessel about to be boarded by lonely me.

Only to find my next surprise.

The door to the cabin, which I was quite sure I'd left locked, stood ajar. My first impulse was to jump aboard, storm the cabin, catch the trespasser in the act, and kick the crap out of him, à la McGee, for violating my last vestige of personal space. But in truth, at this point, I wasn't close to being Travis McGee. I wasn't a combat vet who knew about sneak attacks and choke-holds and guns. Didn't I wish. I was an *English teacher* who jogged. I mean, would McGee launch an assault armed only with a Bic ballpoint? Get real.

So I stopped myself from making a foolish, perhaps even fatal, mistake. I controlled my mounting rage, my reckless territorial instincts, and instead took a step back, listening carefully, searching for shadowy movements in the darkness of the boat cabin. But only little waves sloshing around the pilings in the night breeze and the clang-rattle of flagpole lines and mast halyards disturbed the dock's calm. There seemed to be no shapes changing the shadows inside the cabin, no one still aboard.

I climbed quietly down onto the deck and stuck out my right foot, using the toe of my topsider to ease the cabin door back, then fully open. My actions generated no consequences. I was alone. And feeling rudely violated because I smelled smoke, secondhand cigarette smoke, a stench I'm acutely sensitive to because, as a state employee working in a "smoke-free environment," I'm virtually never around tobacco. Not even on potty patrol at Hoover, where sensors have scared the smokers outside. And I detest the smell so much that I avoid it completely in my civilian life, too.

I stepped fully inside the cabin and flipped on the galley light, then opened all the side windows to let in fresh air. I scanned the scene. Everything in the forecabin seemed surprisingly untouched, exactly where I'd left it. From the cabin door to amidships, however, a methodical search had been conducted. All the cabinet doors and drawers lay open and much of their contents had been strewn around the floor. What had the intruder/intruders been looking for now? Why had they stopped with the job only half done? Had I interrupted him/her, scared them off? If so, who had spotted me in time to warn someone else of my approach? Were they still aboard, for godsake?! I banged my fist on the console, snapping my gaze in all directions.

Another quick scan revealed that at least the cabin hadn't been *abusively* vandalized. I turned to inspect the cabin door. The lock appeared intact as well. There was no sign of forced entry. Yet I remained positive I'd left the cabin door locked.

I checked the head, the V-berth, the aft storage compartment, any place big enough to hide a human being, even a very small human being. But again, I found nothing. Next, I examined the hiding spot under the sink where I kept my cash. All was well there, too. So, what had been the objective?

I should have been more scared than outraged, but now I felt only irritated and confused. What, I wondered, were he/they looking for? Then the obvious became manifest—the little padded envelope with the duplicate cassette tape, the backup to the already stolen original. I had left it and "EC's" letter on the dinette table, and now somebody who was afraid of Parnell or the tape or the past had taken both and pulled me further into a definite *plot*. Obviously, I needed to get moving again. And the fact that my dockage time in Sister Bay was up became suddenly a good thing. On the other hand, I was hesitant to leave Kelly Shelberg behind.

At the moment, with noplace else to go, I could only explore the entire vessel once more, then lock up tight till morning. This time I would tie the door shut from the *inside* with a thick nylon anchor cord. Again, I considered calling the cops, reporting this latest "crime," but their questions could lead to more and I'd be forced to give information about a mysterious cassette tape and deathbed letters and ancient tragedies. I might even be labeled a "person of interest" regarding Parnell's demise.

So, after securing my quarters, I made myself think of other things. Like how, before cruising off the next day, I would find Kelly and ask if we could meet again later next week. The first opportunity I'd have to rent another prime slip at this marina would be in five or six days.

Eventually, I clutched my way to an uneasy sleep thinking how, like MacDonald's McGee, I should install some kind of elaborate alarm system aboard my boat, something that warned me of intruders, something with flashing lights and sirens screaming, not singing.

Early, *very* early the next morning, I was up and waiting for Kelly to report for work at Al Johnson's. I waited only five minutes because she drove in a good ten minutes before her shift began. Just enough time for a quick conversation.

"Looks like you're still a morning person," she commented pleasantly.

"Got the boot. My slip's been rented."

Kelly didn't reply, offering me a puzzled look instead, the facial equivalent of "Yeah, and . . . ?"

"I can get another spot next week. So I'm wondering if you'd like to take off some afternoon when the weather's good and do a little cruising?"

She didn't smile. "I guess," she answered with obvious unease.

"Or would that be just too spooky?"

"You mean because it was Jimmy's boat?"

"Who?"

"*Jimmy.* You know, Charles James Parnell. He went by his middle name."

"Uh-huh," I managed, thinking: *Holy shit!* Recalling nearly in full the "Dear Jimmy" letter I'd had in my possession just twelve hours earlier. I was glad once more that I'd kept copious notes on its contents. And I knew those notes were safe.

Then Kelly continued, breaking the spell of "EC's" echoing words on my roving attention. "But that's not it, really," she said. "It's, well . . . you know, I want to be cautious."

"Sorry. Didn't mean to push."

She paused a moment, thinking over what I'd said. "When you get back, call me and we'll see how we feel."

"It's a hypothetical date, then?"

"A floating commitment," she clarified.

She took a scrap of paper from her purse and wrote down her phone number, handing it to me and saying, "Here. It's unlisted and now I've gotta run or I'll be late, okay? You be careful."

"I'll try," I answered, wondering what she was referring to: *Be careful.*

"Where are you going?"

"Not far. Island hopping mostly—Chambers, Washington, St. Martin, maybe over to Upper Michigan for a day, wherever the impulse leads me and wherever I can find the easiest, safest anchorage. I'll try calling you if I can find an open slip at a full-service marina."

"No cell phone?"

"Low-tech guy in a high-tech world."

"Well, do your best!" She touched my forearm, sending her sensory charge though my system yet again. "See ya."

"I hope" was all I could manage.

Before leaving, I also wanted to call on Nelson Brite and find out what he knew about Parnell's connection to a local punk named Bruder. Or to an old man who died by drowning two decades back. Brite seemed the logical one to give me a detailed update on Door County history and culture since he seemed to be writing about it regularly and thoughtfully. But right now I needed to be gone a while, away from burglars, alone at sea, freely afloat.

By noon I was underway and enjoying very favorable conditions—a gentle southwest wind and nearly flat seas. I started by cruising out to nearby Chambers Island, a three-mile by two-mile area that was once the site of a thriving community in the previous century, according to Brite. Following Brite's recommendation in *Super Sail*, I made the twelve-mile trip, planning to anchor for a day and night in the large harbor at the north end of the island, which contained "a very fine sand beach."

I had succeeded with one important errand before pulling out of Sister Bay. I found a box of what the variety store clerk called "nearly extinct" continuous-feed computer paper, a thousand sheets, all connected end to end with "extra fine perforation," which also held in place the gear-punched feeder strips along the sides. The whole box was cheaper than a hundred sheets of classic typing bond stationery, and, once I'd removed the feeder strips, I could set up my little Smith Corona to operate Kerouac-like, in imitation of that restless roamer who supposedly tapped out *On the Road* in an inspired three-week rush, a 120-foot roll of teletype paper.

Right now the Smith Corona was hidden where I'd found it—deep in the V-berth storage area, under my thick poncho. With the typewriter were the pages of notes I'd made from carefully reviewing the backup tape. I'd folded the sheets and placed them in the typewriter case, tucking them under the portable. The cassette-tape thief had failed to discover either the Smith Corona or my notes, which constituted a veritable transcript of the conversations on the tape and the letter from "EC" to Jimmy.

Later that day, with *Siren Song* holding well, anchored comfortably just off Chambers Island, with the skipper lounging on the aft deck, warming in the sun and occasionally staring across the water at the inviting beach that Brite had so accurately described, I let myself become engrossed in another Travis McGee mystery. McGee and an old girlfriend are aboard McGee's barge-like 52-foot houseboat, *The Busted Flush*, when the girl opens a package that turns out to be a crude bomb. And McGee suffers another traumatic beating. Soon I was thinking: 1) Why hadn't I myself considered the possibility that my mystery envelope might have been a bomb, and 2) This man McGee could really take a hit. I recalled how in other books McGee had been shot, stabbed, clubbed, punched, kicked—again and again—and still managed to come back for more. Must have had a *very* high threshold of pain and a helluva healthcare plan, featuring a terrific physical therapist.

And, of course, McGee survived the bombing, though the ex-girlfriend didn't. And that brought another topic to the forefront: McGee and his women friends. The man really went through 'em, for all sorts of reasons, in all kinds of weather and circumstances. I had, by now, lost count of McGee's conquests. Was it forty-something? More? McGee even used sexual healing as part of his bomb recovery therapy. Another world.

I began to feel restless, the thought of bombed boats, tempting women, and threatening intruders taking a strong hold on *my* imagination. So I hauled out the dinghy and rowed to the beach, where I spent an hour relaxing on the sand. From the shore, I thought my boat looked quite impressive. It had nice lines, a clean appearance, and I felt proud to be the owner, Chevrolet or not.

The rest of the reasonably calm day and evening and night I spent reading. I laid aside McGee to dip into one of the Nelson Brite books I'd purchased. It was a collection of essays entitled *Appropriations*, mainly about his experiences as a local writer and occasional teacher. I found a piece called "The Best Writer's Workshop Ever!" and one line from the introduction leaped out at me: "My lively, diverse group included the peninsula's most successful great-grandmother/playwright, Vivian Stanton, as well as tough cop/story writer Jim Parnell." I could barely swallow as I raced through the short article. Unfortunately, there was just one other mention of Parnell: "And like some others in the group, Jim Parnell often uses incidents from local history as inspiration for his work. 'Starting points,' he calls them."

I tried reading two more selections but couldn't stay with them. My mind was racing. I put aside Brite and tried to calm myself down by organizing a float plan for the next day. I hoped to anchor in Detroit Island's Pedersen Bay. From there I thought it possible to get over to Washington Island by dinghy, the channel separating the two islands being fairly narrow and shallow, but still a good little row. On the island I was sure to find the pay phone that could connect me with Nelson Brite. I'd finally accepted the fact that pretending nothing was happening around me (and to me) was futile escapism. Sooner or later I would have to take an active role in discovering the meaning of all the baggage I'd acquired with the purchase of Parnell's boat.

I would have to ask somebody, probably Brite:

1) Who was/is Raymond Bruder?

2) Who was/is Kay Farrow?

3) How was Parnell connected to Bruder and Farrow?

4) Who is/was "EC"?

5) Who was the "old guy" Bruder had mentioned, the one who drove off the Northport dock and into the lake?

6) Exactly what local history had Parnell written about?

Before tidying up the cabin and turning in for the night, I took another inventory of the MacDonald titles. I'd been flying through the collection much too quickly for it to last the summer, let alone the month of June. What I needed was to pace myself. So I emptied the box of books, intending to put the novels I'd already completed at the bottom, leaving the unread titles on the top layers for easier access. And it was when I had lifted out the last of the JDM books that I discovered my next *Siren Song* stunner.

The book box labeled USED PARTS had, I discerned, a clever but obviously home-crafted false bottom. And what I found hidden in the "secret" space created by the previous owner suddenly made my detective work momentous.

CHAPTER 10

The false bottom offered a compartment where Parnell, I assume, had stashed a collection of 10 × 13–inch manila envelopes. The first one I opened contained a batch of newspaper clippings, all neatly cut and stapled, taken from many different years, all about the wintertime death of an elderly farmer named Harold Sloan. I quickly scanned the top article and the oldest—published nearly twenty years earlier—a rather ambitious overview of the "accident." Somehow, between the lines of the newspaper story, the words recorded on the taped Q&A excerpts I had listened to echoed in my mind.

DEATH'S DOOR DROWNING REMAINS A MYSTERY

In the year since Harold Sloan, a seventy-nine-year-old retired Brown County farmer, was found dead in his car under eighteen feet of water off the Northport ferry dock, investigators have learned almost nothing about exactly when and how the accident occurred and why Sloan had driven to the tip of the Door County peninsula. A contingent of *relatives still claims that Sloan was tricked into leaving his home, then murdered for his money. They speculate that Sloan might very well have been carrying as much as $100,000 to $150,000 when he left his home for the last time, as he had supposedly been liquidating his assets for months. However, when Sloan's Ford Galaxy was pulled from the near freezing waters off the 325' concrete Northport Pier, he had only about $8,000 with him, most of it in $100, $50, and $20 bills. The other cash assets have never been located or satisfactorily accounted for.*

Sloan, who was thought to be in the early stages of Alzheimer's disease, had mentioned to a niece that he had a "new special friend," apparently a woman he had somehow met over the phone. The identity of the woman friend remains unknown. While local chief investigator Robin Graves is guardedly optimistic that the suspicious death will eventually be solved, Sloan's relatives seem quite certain that time has now run out. A niece of Sloan's stated: "Someone has gotten away with murder and thousands of dollars of untraceable money."

Had Parnell been an investigating officer? I wondered. No, not possible. The tape of the interview between a cop and a hood was made nearly ten years after the drowning. Twenty years earlier Parnell wouldn't have been old enough to have been a policeman, maybe about seventeen at the time. Then I recalled the cop on the tape saying: "I was in high school."

So Parnell had evidently become obsessed for some reason with this unsolved case early in his career and discovered a conspiracy on his own. A pattern of collusion was what he seemed to be trying to establish during the taped interviews. Was that it? Was the young cop Parnell attempting to break the Big Case and accelerate his rise up the ladder of command? Could I even be certain that Parnell's was the voice conducting the interviews? So much was so vague, so uncertain, so unclear. Still, I made more notes to myself, listing all the specific names I'd heard mentioned on the tapes—Raymond Bruder, Kay Farrow, Treasure Telemarketing—as well as "EC" the letter writer, and "Brad W," the deceased husband. I would check these all out, I thought, when it occurred to me that already my laid-back summer was as gone as Harold Sloan's money.

If only I had managed to hang on to the duplicate tapes. Then I could have had Kelly Shelberg listen to part of one and tell me if the investigator's voice was Parnell's. Because it now appeared totally obvious that the "JP" addressed on the backup tape package was not me but Jimmy Parnell, a cop who died a death frighteningly similar to that of the old man named in the articles. I then carefully read through the rest of the clippings, all of which emphasized the troublesome nature of Sloan's "accident," the likelihood of foul play, the unexplained, and seemingly unexplainable, disappearance of a great deal of hard cash.

The next papers in the pile looked like personal notes—cryptic and abbreviated lists, directives and claims. One packet, for example, held account records, the sheets full of penciled entries like "4/11—T.S.—6,350 rec val" and "5/9—M&W—11,275 rec val." The notes had been typed on the same antique Smith Corona portable I had recently appropriated for my own journals and note-taking. The giveaway detail was the capital M's whose second peak was often faded, sometimes to near invisibility. The note containing the final faded M stopped me cold: "Monday—CS/Set-up to NB/critique." I lifted that page and underneath found an unsealed 9 × 12 brown envelope addressed to "Nelson Brite, Re: Workshop Story." But that neat printing had been crossed out with a black felt-tip marker and replaced by a hastily written "Back at ya, Jim!"

Now buzzingly wide awake, I reached into the open envelope and found a manuscript, which Parnell had entitled "Champagne Shuffle." There were nine and a half pages of straight narration followed by a crude outline made up of several vague headings: "Plus five update, Background RR, Transfer/Payroll/Calls, Endgame." The first few manuscript pages contained comments from Brite in the margins. Anxiously, I began:

CHAMPAGNE SHUFFLE

The old man was lost, driving his champagne-colored Ford Galaxy through fog then snow, working his way northeast, right up the bay side of the Door County peninsula. He was supposed to meet her in one of the towns along the way, but he couldn't remember anymore exactly which one she said. So he kept on driving, thinking maybe he'd recognize the name when he saw it. But soon he had covered nearly the entire peninsula and nothing seemed familiar. He wanted to find her. He'd brought her what she wanted, all of it, small bills just like she'd asked.

Quickly, I judged that all the author was doing thus far was summarizing what he'd taken from the newspaper articles. Was Parnell trying to be another John D. MacDonald with his color-coded title (*Champagne!*) taken right from the journalist's work?

In the left margin, Brite had scribbled: "Money <u>and</u> a girl! Good start!"

Next:

The snow began falling when he was just north of Sturgeon Bay, and the wet heavy flakes came down harder and faster as he inched his way up the last part of the peninsula—Egg Harbor, Fish Creek, Ephraim, Sister Bay, Ellison Bay, Gills Rock. None of the names meant anything. He couldn't recall anymore what she'd said. Only that she needed him and would really appreciate his help. So he was bringing the money, absolutely all of it, everything he had, knowing, in a sense, that it was all very strange, a young girl like that snuggling up to him, nearly eighty and becoming forgetful. But he was so lonely, he missed Katherine so much for the last few years, that when the girl showed up on his doorstep one day, he couldn't help himself.

To which Brite responded: "Katherine is the <u>wife</u>, I suppose? Clarify. And <u>eighty</u>? Maybe too old for romance?"
   Then:

She said she was taking a survey and Algoma was her territory. So they sat down in his parlor and she began asking him all kinds of questions about what it felt like to be retired. She asked how he spent his time and how he paid his bills. When the talk turned to money, he had to brag a little. He'd always lived very carefully and had sold some of his land and equipment at just the right times for the best possible prices.

It seemed to me the narrative was now taking on a life of its own, to include "facts" not covered by the *Green Bay*

Bulletin articles—like the wife's name, the business about surveys in Algoma.

I continued with renewed interest:

> *And the girl said she wished she could be independent, too. She wanted to start her own business. She needed to get away from the abusive boyfriend who got drunk sometimes and hit her. She even hiked up her skirt enough to show him a small bruise on her thigh. He took it all in, the beautiful long leg, the whole show.*
>
> *Soon they were laughing a lot together, and that's when she asked him for funding to get her business started. And he said, "Sure!" So they made plans to meet at . . . at . . . Dammit! He still couldn't remember, though he was certain he must have written it down someplace, maybe typed it on a card or something.*

With Brite interjecting: "<u>Drunk, abusive boyfriend</u>? Too stock/clichéd? More individualizing development needed?"

Parnell went on:

> *She was going to show him the building and business she wanted to buy way the hell up the peninsula, and he was going to back her financially, be a sort of silent partner. And why the hell not? His own children, both married now with families of their own, living far away, so far they never even phoned anymore except at Christmas, they didn't seem to need him. So to hell with them! And some of the relatives still close by scared him sometimes, like that Rudy, always wanting a handout. But she was here now, in the flesh and beautiful and friendly, and she needed him, his help. If only he could find her. God, he wanted to find her, make her smile again. He wanted to <u>mean</u> something to her.*

At this point, perhaps contrary to Brite (who had written "<u>Credible</u>?!?" about five times in *both* margins), I was beginning to care about these characters.

Reading again:

> *Then he saw another sign: Northport. Still no glimmer of recognition, no jog of memory. What the hell was the name of that town?! The snow rushing down now, covering the pines, laying heavily, wetly on the low-hanging boughs. He pushed on, following a twisting, turning, slippery roadway, moving even more slowly on the icy pavement, all alone on the road, worried about sliding off into the trees, crashing and missing her altogether, maybe even getting himself hurt.*
>
> *And then he arrived at the end of the road, at least that's the way it looked through the blowing snow. Maybe it was a bridge. Strangely, he had never been up this far before, not being a hunter or fisherman or vacationer. He continued to stare down at the structure extending before him into the darkness, unable to see the end of it. He came to a full stop. He rolled down his window to try for a better look, his windshield wipers barely able to move away the heavy snow.*
>
> *Then he heard it, an engine, whining, coming closer. Two engines. He glanced in his rear-view mirror but could see nothing through the layers of accumulated snow. He tried his side mirror and then saw the headlights bouncing along, moving in close. Snowmobiles. He remained stopped, his engine starting to idle roughly. And soon they were next to him, dismounting from their sleds, stepping closer to his car. Two of them.*
>
> *The first called out through the howling wind and snow, "You lost?"*

The wind screaming, tearing at his face through the open side window, pulling tears from his eyes. "Can't find her!" the old man hollered into the wind. "Can't remember!"

"Remember what?" yelled back the first, fully raising the helmet visor.

The old man peered at the young face inside the helmet, so young, and decided it wasn't her. Then the old man shouted, "This the way to the next town?" Pointing through his windshield. Where was he?

Following this section, which ended halfway down the page, the rest left blank, Brite had summarized: "Strong sensory details effectively evoke ominous mood! Characterization needs tighter focus and relationships portrayed sometimes threaten to defy credibility. But there is a solid story here ready to emerge, a story worth telling. Go for it, Jim!"

And those were the last of Brite's comments, so I assumed he had never seen what I was about to read. I refocused on the manuscript, turning to the next page:

The other looked at the one with the raised visor, and both shook their heads. But then the one whose face he couldn't see, the much taller and bigger one, began nodding, then raised the helmet visor just enough to holler, "Sure mister! Straight ahead! Can't miss it!" The open-faced one laughing suddenly, reeling back and forth. And before either one of the snowmobilers could say anything else, the old man shifted the champagne Galaxy into gear and drove onto the ice-packed surface of the Northport Ferry Dock, gaining speed even as his car jounced wildly over the ridges of ice, like

*he was racing his old farm truck down a stretch of rail-
road ties.*

Here I could imagine Brite repeating his compliment
about "strong sensory details." There were plenty of
them. But details offered in the name of . . . *what* exactly? Where was this thing going? I wondered. Where
would it lead?

*Finally, he arrived at the very end of the road, the end
of the pier, and he could see that. He jammed on his
brakes but not soon enough. His front wheels dropped
over the edge and soon the bulky sedan's rear end was
swinging slowly around, sending more and more of the
chassis out over the ice-covered water. He looked back at
the snowmobilers who seemed frozen in place, standing
there like statues.*

*With his car continuing to slide gradually but
steadily over the end of the pier, passenger side first, the
old man pushed open his door and tossed out two plastic bags. Then he pushed out the encased little machine
he'd brought for her, to help with the business corre-
spondence. He was hauling up the last bag, an old
leather briefcase, boxy and full, from behind the seat
when the car's position shifted dramatically, tipping
slowly, grinding and grating toward the frozen lake,
then rolling over so quickly that the driver's side door
slammed shut on him just as he dumped the briefcase,
banging his head. He was trapped in the car now, and
it was taking him into the lake, the bone-chilling crash
through the ice floes knocking him senseless, the freezing
water quickly dulling his nervous system, killing him
almost instantly.*

Reading that, I actually shivered. Then rushed to the finish:

> *At the near end of the dock the boy and girl watched in horror. They couldn't believe it. They'd said one dumb, drunken, sarcastic, stupid thing, and the old guy raced off before they could take it back, and now he was probably dead!*
>
> *The girl was the first to scream. No longer drunk, no longer warm and flush from the passionate clinging love she'd just shared with the boy, doing it again and again in the cabin where neither one of them was supposed to be that weekend, she jumped on her sled and gestured frantically for the boy to follow, get the hell out of there now! But he waved her on, signaled for her to go first and get out of sight. When she had disappeared into the howling snow, racing around the first turn of the twisting road, the boy stumbled down to the far end of the pier to see if the old man was really a goner. On the way he looked back, scanning the shore, checking for lights in any of the homes and cottages along the stoney beach, any witnesses. It was so late. There shouldn't have been any lights on and there weren't.*

Sex and violence, love and death, money and corruption. They were all here, I judged.

Concluding:

> *At the far end of the dock the boy discovered what the old man had thrown from his car. With the snow pounding at him even harder now, the wind gnawing and shrieking dangerously, the boy took one cautious glance over the end of the pier and that was enough to tell him*

*all he needed to know. The old man's car had sunk with-
out a trace. In fact, the ice floes were sliding and shifting
so wildly now in the high wind that the boy dared to hope
maybe there was enough of a current to pull the car way
out into the lake where it might never be found. But there
were still the bags to deal with, and that little black case
with the handle.*

*Awkwardly, the boy scooped them all up. He would
hide them. He would put them someplace where nobody
would think to look, where nobody would expect to find
them. He would then catch up to the girl. He would convince her to never ever say anything to anyone about this
thing that had just happened, ever! And he wouldn't tell
anyone about what the old man had left on the dock.*

*So, clutching the case and bags, he climbed on his sled
and rode off slowly toward a great hiding place.*

And that was it, all the writing Parnell had left behind
. . . I think. And Brite had missed the best of it. I inhaled
deeply. Parnell's story intrigued me, scared me, but how
much was fiction? How much was fact?

Before allowing myself some desperately desired
sleep, I chose instead to review the entire collection of
documents—all the notes, the articles, the story frag-
ments and bits of dialogue appearing on other pages,
the whole package. And it wasn't long before I saw troublesome patterns forming while focusing on certain details. Like how Parnell could have been that kid in the
story. He would have been the right age when Sloan
died. But if Parnell himself was the culprit, then why was
he trying to implicate Bruder and Farrow?

At last, exhausted, I hoped to drop off for a few hours
of sleep. The following morning I had planned to cruise

the waters around St. Martin Island and then go all the way to Michigan's Upper Peninsula, the Big Bay de Noc region, but come back to Detroit Island for the night. The way I felt now, though, it seemed likely that the pleasure boating would be cut short, would have to wait, because the first order of business was to get to a phone and track down the names I'd collected from listening to the cassette tape and reading through Parnell's notes. I reviewed some crucial parts of Parnell's story: "he pushed out the encased little machine . . . hauling up the last bag, an old leather briefcase . . . the boy scooped them all up . . . would hide them."

Then I thought to add Nelson Brite to my must-call list, since he was clearly involved. I would ask him about Parnell's writing, whether he'd ever submitted the full text of "Champagne Shuffle" or not. And if Brite wondered why I'd become so interested in Parnell so quickly, I would answer:

1) I own the man's boat.

2) I've already met and dated his ex.

3) I just spotted his name in the first essay of yours that I've read.

4) I found your comments on his manuscript.

5) I looked him in the face moments before he died.

And I would end with "Mr. Brite, can't you see the stunning confluence of coincidences here? Do you have a key role in this drama? Do you have any other Parnell manuscripts? Am I already lost in something I can't handle?"

I suffered through another near-sleepless night.

CHAPTER 11

The following day—edgy, sleep-starved, *excited*—I cruised directly to Detroit Island beneath cloudy skies, through light chop. To get to Detroit and Washington Islands I had to cross the ominously named Porte des Morts Strait, Death's Door Passage. This channel has always been dangerous because the differences in water temperature between Green Bay and Lake Michigan sometimes create strong currents that run counter to the wind, currents that can spin boats around or send them bottoming onto the detached reefs and shoals surrounding the channel islands. Many of those two hundred–plus area shipwrecks happened because of Death's Door. In fact, the famous French pioneer/fur trader, Robert LaSalle, was last seen back in 1679 leaving Washington Island and going into Porte des Morts aboard his ship . . . the *Griffin.*

Fortunately, my motorized passage was uneventful. *Siren Song* cut smoothly through the rippling seas, and I had no sooner cleared the strait, entered Detroit Island's

Pedersen Bay, found darker, blue-green water I could trust, and set my anchor than I was in the dinghy, rowing vigorously with its little oars across the open water separating me from Washington Island.

The entire way over, I thought again about the police, about whether or not now was the time to finally call them in. Yet if I did call, what could I give them but a story, my word that some incriminating, mysterious audiotapes had existed, had certainly proven thought-provoking, and had been stolen? And what did I imagine Parnell had given me to report? Hard facts that could build a real case? Not really. Just a lot of suggestive details, too many of which seemed dreadfully self-incriminating for Parnell, if not absolutely self-damning. And none appeared absolutely factual.

One of the most condemning of the documents included in these files, if it were indeed an authentic text, was a partial letter, typed on Sloan's personal stationery it appeared, an error-ridden few sentences of a first-draft note to a "Miss S." The thoughts expressed were anonymous, mundane—"*Mighty cold this morning, but feel good. Maybe later in the week we can have coffee*" and so on—but what caught my eye almost immediately were all of the one-peaked M's scattered throughout the text. So the Smith Corona that Parnell (and now I myself) "owned" had once been the property (the "little machine") of this guy Sloan? A machine housed in the case that the old man had thrown from his car? Wouldn't that obviously make Parnell "the boy" present at that horrible death scene? But if Parnell could be judged here as admitting his involvement in Sloan's death and revealing his guilt, where did Raymond Bruder and Kay Farrow fit in?

Even more amazing: If Parnell, a cop, really was an inadvertent killer, how could he be so careless or arrogant as to leave such sensitive information aboard his boat? Did he really think he could get away with writing and perhaps publishing a story based on a death he appeared to be deeply involved with, even identified professionally with? Or had he simply tried to use writing as therapy—a way to work out or work off his guilt? And how could Parnell imagine that Bruder, Farrow et al. would somehow fail to notice if he were to actually get the thing published? What about Sloan's disgruntled relatives? Or EC? Did Parnell know at the time he was working on his story that his old lover would not be alive long enough to hurt him? Or was this entire mystery *pure fiction*, Parnell's imagined construct peopled only by ghosts and fakes?

Rowing harder now, looking back at a fully loaded car ferry easing up to the docks, I knew I had to ascertain exactly how much of what Parnell had left me was absolute factual truth. How much mere fabrication. Again, I went back to the missing tapes, thinking: Suppose it was Parnell doing the questioning. Did that make the tapes authentic? Was Parnell actually being a cop on those tapes? Or could he have been merely *playing* a cop, doing a little "cop theater" just to see how well the dialogue worked for his writing project? Hadn't Parnell surrounded himself with mystery novels? Didn't the hero of nearly all of them, Travis McGee, play a variety of parts to get what he wanted, to protect himself in difficult circumstances? I mean, McGee posed as a police investigator, a lawyer, a claims adjuster, a photo lens repairman, etc. etc. So couldn't Parnell be seen as a Travis wannabe? But if the entire tape was pure theater, why would anybody need to steal not one but two copies?

Next, I thought of "EC" whose letter accompanied the second tape when it arrived at my door—she appeared put off by the cassette. Had Parnell perhaps forgotten to include with his original mailing some message explaining his actions, that most basic of communication courtesies, the *cover letter*? But if the tape depressed and alienated "EC," reminded her of old mischief, wouldn't the secret she was so proud of keeping be the "fact" that she witnessed Parnell's involvement in a stormy December death scene over twenty years before?

And how could I fail to perceive at that moment the horrible parallel irony of Parnell's own death by water? The circumstances of his "accident" were just as clouded as Sloan's, maybe criminally so.

And what of my own connections to Parnell? Truly, it was as though I were trading my life for his. Wasn't I living aboard his boat, reading and relishing his books, chasing his dreams, falling already half in love with his ex-wife? So couldn't the person or persons breaking into my boat now consider *me* their new enemy? Some guy who's purposefully taking up where Parnell had left off? Some guy who already knows too much about what they might be trying to get . . . or to conceal? Because if the tapes thief thought I had listened to the cassette and fully understood it, wouldn't I clearly be in far more danger than even I cared to think? So it was imperative that I find out *right now* if Bruder and Farrow are/were real people and not mere characters in Parnell's Q&A sketch.

As I continued grunting and pulling against the current, I realized how vulnerable I'd become. Not just because I was all alone bouncing a dinghy across a typically busy boat channel, but because of *Siren Song*, all the menacing mystery. Living with Margot was difficult sometimes, especially at the end, but it was never dangerous.

Then another thought crossed my mind, causing me to ship my oars: What if the people pursuing Parnell through me (or pursuing me outright) were law enforcement types? What if someone in authority had suspicions or concerns about Parnell and had discovered enough to consider him a threat, a loose cannon that could embarrass the department, or even implicate his peers in something sinister? Was he a significant witness who had to be silenced? What had that TV reporter said about "an internal investigation" at Green Bay Police headquarters? My imagination was running wild. I covered the last yards to shore in near panic, rowing like some single sculler seeking a gold medal.

Finally, I tied my dinghy to a short dock right behind a shed squeezed between two small commercial buildings. Then I climbed onto the dock, scanned the area, and quickly located a public phone. I was also lucky to have the privacy of a phone booth. My first call was to Information, and after doing a "regional search," the operator reported to me that there were no listings in the area for either a Raymond Bruder or a Kay Farrow. "And nothing on Nelson Brite," she added. Unlisted? I wondered. Certainly not phoneless. Cell phone user exclusively?

Next, recalling from the tapes that Bruder had supposedly been a guy with a record who had perhaps done prison time, I dared to phone the Green Bay Police again and got absolutely nowhere, all such information and details being "sealed and confidential due to privacy laws and accessible only to certified law enforcement personnel and criminal justice officials. And who are you anyway?" At the last second, I thought to ask about "Robin Graves," the police investigator mentioned in the first newspaper article I'd read from Parnell's files. "Retired years ago and went to Alaska," the desk man replied. "Why do you want to know?" I hung up.

Then I tried the regional newspapers, hoping to find out if they had ever carried, or presently carried, a "crime section," one of those columns that reports the statistics of violence and misbehavior, summarizing the outcomes of local court cases—listing offenders arrested, their alleged crimes, their official sentences. The student intern at the *Green Bay Bulletin* who took my call left me on hold for nearly five minutes—five that seemed like fifty, me scratching my arms and legs in the still, humid air of the bug-infested booth. Lots of flies and mosquitos and semi-conscious moths for company. I shooed a good many of them out and snapped the door shut.

At last, the young man returned to report: "Sorry, but nothing came up on the computer for those names, but hey, I s'pose I coulda screwed it up. But I don't think so, cuz I'm pretty handy with software."

"Uh-huh," I mumbled, thinking: Could both Bruder and Farrow be dead or gone, too?

My next call went to the Green Bay public school system's central office. Representing myself as an out-of-town feature writer doing a follow-up profile on the "fine young police officer who recently died so tragically and needlessly," I was able to soon learn that Parnell was a graduate of Green Bay East High School, had in fact been quite a big-time athlete there in his day.

From Green Bay East, I was lucky enough to find a *friendly* secretary working the main desk who told me that summer school was in session and that she was "really very busy," but that she could do me "one small favor," considering the purpose of my inquiry. I had asked her to please take out the yearbooks from Parnell's junior and senior years. Every high school I had ever entered had a full set of yearbooks in some closet near the principal's office so that "culprit identification and apprehension" could be made efficiently and swiftly.

When the secretary came back on the line and announced that she had the relevant annuals in her hands, giving me the school years covered, I figured that Parnell could indeed have been "the boy" dramatized in his story fragment; the ages were just right. Parnell would have been seventeen exactly twenty years earlier, the year of Sloan's death.

Then the secretary asked me what I wanted to know specifically, so I requested that she list Parnell's accomplishments, as clearly documented in the yearbook, in the areas of sports (lots of pictures, she said, long captions, many individual awards), student government (very little information—he'd been a "second vice-president of the Letterman's Club," whatever that meant), academics (even less detail—he'd been no Merit Scholar), social activities, such as homecoming royalty? *Why, yes!* His senior year Parnell and his girlfriend were on the homecoming court, the secretary reported. "Cute couple," she added.

Then I dared to ask, "What's the girlfriend's name?"

"Erin Chilton. A beautiful girl. And a fine athlete herself, it looks like."

"Uh-huh," I said, satisfied by my finally having a full proper name for the mystery woman "EC." I was about to thank the secretary for her help and hang up but stopped myself in time to ask about one more East High grad. "I'm also looking for the full name of a friend of the officer's and all I have is 'Brad W.'"

I could hear her sigh and start flipping pages.

"There are three," she reported. "In that class, I mean."

"Three Brad Ws?"

"Yes. You want them all?"

"If I could, please."

"Well, there's Brad Watts, Brad Wilhelm, and Brad Wychoff."

"Is that last one W-y-c-h-o-v?"

"O-f-f," she clarified.

"Thanks so much. You've been a *big* help," I said.

"My pleasure. I'll be looking for that article," she replied before hanging up.

So EC lives, I thought. Then catching myself: *lived.* From her letter, it was pretty clear she didn't have long. That would be another detail worth checking. But under what name had she been living down there in Florida? Her married? Her maiden? And if she were already dead . . .

Still, I had to do the right thing and *try.* She had mentioned Pensacola in her letter, so I rang up the Naval Air Station (NAS) there and, posing as an insurance claims manager, requested information about a Brad W, "former aircrewman." I further explained that Brad W was deceased, having been killed in an automobile accident, and that we couldn't find his last name accurately recorded anywhere.

"The agent who did the paperwork on this originally just abbreviated the name throughout. But we think it could be Watts, Wilhelm, or Wychoff," I speculated. "The widow is using her maiden name."

"Why do you want to know all this?" the administrator demanded. "I mean, why don't you just ask this man's widow?"

"Well, she's quite ill, virtually incapacitated, and can't be bothered. All we're trying to do is determine if she's entitled to any additional benefit, however slight, from her husband's military insurance. We're just trying to do the right thing here," I added, in my most appeasing voice.

There was an anxious pause before the NAS administrator informed me that "any such privileged information on non-commissioned personnel was strictly *confidential* and *classified* and *inaccessible* over the phone. So please submit your request in writing," he ordered. Asshole.

The last call I'd planned on making was to the area Small Business Administration. I wanted to see if they'd ever heard of Treasure Telemarketing. After being transferred to three different bureaucrats, I learned that none of them had "any information on, or record of, such an operation," nor would they "be disposed to discuss such an operation if it did in fact exist, without proper authorization." One even asked me to spell the company name. So that was that, end of inquiry. And still no way to connect quickly with Brite.

Angry and frustrated, I was about to give up when I recalled another name worth checking out, one Victor Colby of Two Rivers, Wisconsin, the semi driver who had actually pushed Parnell off Tower Drive Bridge. Was there any reason to doubt his testimony?

Not according to his wife or his boss, whose number Mrs. Colby gave me just in case I doubted *her* word. "I know you reporters," she'd said. Victor Colby, it turned out, was a thirty-year veteran trucker who had never had a single accident or received a single traffic ticket. The Parnell incident "really shook him up," reported his employer, but they'd been able to talk him back into the cab and onto the road. "He seems a little better," said the boss.

And I was finished. I would find Brite later. I went back to my dinghy and cast off.

I aimed myself at *Siren Song*, gripping the short oars tightly and really putting my back into it, pulling hard and evenly. Fifty strokes into the journey, I glanced at my boat to check my bearings, and that's when I spotted the guy coming out of the cabin door—short, skinny, dark-haired, dressed in a T-shirt, jeans, running shoes, one foot on the gunwale, standing in profile, as if he was about to step off onto another boat (one I couldn't see) rafted alongside mine, cigarette hanging lazily from his lips.

Ridiculously, more annoyed than afraid, I hollered across the water: "Hey! HEY!! The hell you *doin'*?!" Breaking the rhythm of my rowing, sending myself off course, enraged that I could only watch helplessly as the intruder, empty-handed, spotted me, then disappeared over the far side of *Siren Song.*

Soon I heard the cough and gurgle of a cranking marine engine. Instantly, the throttle was opened wide and a runabout raced off, pounding away across the water, heading southeast through the channel toward Lake Michigan and quickly away from me. The boat, I was frustrated to see, was almost perfectly generic in appearance, looking like lots of other new fiberglass inboards that summer—white hull, dark turquoise-green trim, white seats. Nothing set this one apart. I glared at his wake as I drifted in the current.

Back aboard *Siren Song,* I discovered that the methodical search begun in Sister Bay was now complete—the forward half of my boat had been recklessly ransacked, but again I didn't think anything was missing. The book box had been pulled from the V-berth storage bin and opened, but only the top layers of JDM paperbacks had been taken out and left scattered on the deck. Everything hidden in the false bottom—Parnell's notes, his story, the clippings—was still in place, just as I'd left it. The typewriter had been left undisturbed, too. What was the guy after this time? Who the hell *was* he?

As I cleaned up the mess, checking carefully for anything lost, I reflected that unlike last time, I couldn't be sure I'd locked up my boat before setting off for Washington Island. I probably hadn't, I'd been in such a hurry to get ashore. And now it was imperative to get moving again. The trouble was I didn't have a clue where to go, where I could anchor or tie up and feel safe. Because it was crystal clear now that someone was watching me and my boat at all times, and was having no trouble following my schedule.

I ran the blowers and started the engine, then pulled the anchor and headed out of Pedersen Bay, making a token effort at pursuing my tormentor, even though I knew my chances of finding and confronting him were minimal . . . and in a way I was glad. The plot was thickening much too quickly now for my taste.

Leaving Washington Island waters, I entered Lake Michigan, intending to pass by Rock Island and head back down into Green Bay. But I was running without the one thing Kriel urged me always to have—a "float plan," a specific idea of where I wanted to go, why I wanted to go there, and how I intended to get there most sensibly. What I needed most, of course, was even more time to sort my situation out, to move and dodge and hide and *think*. I had no clear idea of what I'd stumbled into. With the second search of my boat, was I now safe? The only consolation I could find was that the guy didn't seem to want a physical confrontation any more than I did.

But what did I actually have that he might want? What was valuable enough for him to examine every inch of the boat? Not the old Smith Corona portable, I bet. The only connections between the machine and Sloan were made by Parnell in his fiction, if it was indeed Parnell doing the writing and file making. What if it did turn out that the portable once belonged to Sloan? Perhaps Parnell simply took it from the old man's home as part of a follow-up investigation. Or maybe Parnell had found it gathering dust in some back corner of the Green Bay Police Department's evidence room and thought it would be cool to have. The thief already had the tapes. But he had to be an amateur to just toss stuff around. A savvy, patient professional thief takes what he wants neatly, with minimal effort.

What about The Money? To believe in the existence of it meant accepting the reality of all the other elements too, right? Perhaps I should become Travis McGee myself—a sort of freshwater salvage expert. Only I wasn't so keen on being Travis McGee at the moment. I didn't want other interested parties breaking into my boat again, maybe shooting at me next time, or trying to run me down with their cars, or hitting me in the head with pipes, fists, bombs—breaking my nose, blackening my eyes, scarring my body, loosening my teeth. I think I prefer such violence only in books.

CHAPTER 12

I wandered alone for three days and nights, cruising back and forth across Green Bay, haphazardly veering off one course, making ninety-degree turns to pursue another, sometimes cutting power altogether and just floating, but always on the lookout for following craft, for anyone paying too much attention to me. I constantly scanned the horizon with the modest binoculars I'd brought along, sometimes irrationally spinning around to check my blind sides in the eerie open-water silence.

I spent a short night of fitful sleep anchored off Chambers Island, then followed the western shore of Green Bay all the way to Escanaba, Michigan, anchoring for two more near-sleepless nights in the protected harbor of City Marina. The extensive shoal water running almost the full length of my course didn't help to relax an inexperienced, barely competent skipper like me. And all the while, I was spooked by any vessel operating anywhere close by. Even small aluminum fishing boats with 15-horsepower motors being operated by young kids caused concern. Unlike these Upper Peninsula shoreline waters, paranoia runs far and wide and deep sometimes.

If I'd had a cell phone, I would have tried calling Vesical and talking my situation through with him. He would listen carefully, believing without question that all the fantastic events I'd be narrating had actually happened. He would ask good questions, then thoughtfully list my options. He might even offer a specific course of action or two. But I would have no such therapeutic discussion because once the school year ended, nobody knew for sure where Vesical was. Or if *he* had a cell phone. All summer long the guy raced around the country, making good money judging play competitions, directing short-run summer stock productions, mentoring at playwright workshops. All without a single communication to his best friend from Hoover High.

So my three days adrift passed indistinguishably—the weather continuously overcast, hazy and a bit humid, the winds very light, early dog days. Eventually, I calmed down enough to return to Sister Bay, where I was able to secure a slip for the next twenty-four hours. Early that evening, with *Siren Song* well tied and my supper of cold cuts and cheese finished, the galley cleaned, I walked to the pay phone on Bay Shore Drive and called Kelly Shelberg. All this time alone was making me crazy. I had sweated and paced and muttered, too often and too long.

Kelly's first words were "Hey, I was just thinking about *you*! And then you call? *Perfect.*"

Encouraged by her reaction, I negotiated a meeting time, desperate now for her company. After we'd hung up, I jogged back to my boat, tied the door shut for the night, and read JDM into the wee hours. Trying like hell to pretend everything was sort of normal.

The following morning, a gloriously fresh one, I was waiting on deck at the appointed time, dressed in my best casual, summer, sea-captain garb—white polo shirt, khaki shorts, and topsiders. I broke into a wide smile when I saw Kelly hurrying down the dock, wearing virtually the same outfit, only looking better in it, and carrying a shopping bag in her right arm, gripping a bulky beach duffel with her left. Kelly had agreed to supply the ingredients for our supper aboard *Siren Song*, if I took care of everything else. Watching her approach, I couldn't help contrasting her girlish appeal with the calm, cool demeanor of Margot. Margot never rushed for or after anything, except promotions.

"Ahoy!" Kelly joked. Then, "Hey, we look alike, in uniform."

"Can I give you a hand?" I reached toward her, stepping up on the gunwale.

"I've managed this far," she answered, tossing me her gear and stepping gracefully onto *Siren Song*.

We got ourselves organized. Kelly disappeared into the cabin and put away her provisions and personals. I followed her in to fire up the engine. Then we set free the lines, and I backed *Siren Song* out of her slip.

The day was good, the weather near perfect. It was warm but the breeze had picked up, taking the stagnant humidity with it. The seas looked manageable. The whole world seemed to be beckoning and tranquil.

I had planned to cruise the bayside coastal waters, maybe drop some fishing lines along the way, then troll a course northeast toward Washington Island. But as much as I had liked my anchorage in Pedersen Bay, the thought of being invaded again—this time with Kelly aboard—sent me looking for a romantic harbor elsewhere, and in the opposite direction. Maybe at day's end I would anchor in the well-protected cove of Horseshoe Island, just off Ephraim, supposedly the snuggest harbor in all Green Bay. There one typically drops a stern anchor, rows ashore via dinghy, and ties off the bowline to a tree. The bay is deep enough to get in fairly close to shore, there to be perfectly blocked by the island from troublesome northwest winds.

Our cruise was as close to perfect as I could have hoped. While I operated *Siren Song* from the topside controls, we both *oooohe*d and *aaaahhe*d when passing by dramatic limestone bluffs and cliffs with inviting public beaches lying at the feet of the dolomite outcroppings. Feeling comfortable with the silences, we relaxed in the sun on the command bridge. Then Kelly startled me by shedding her polo shirt and cutting down to a little peach halter top. And when she asked me to help put sunscreen on her back, another of those small intimacies I missed so much, my hand shook as I spread the lotion. A light spray of freckles covered her shoulders, so unlike Margot's dusky perfection.

After we had gone northeast far enough to circle Washington and Rock Islands and had worked our way back down the bay side of the peninsula to Ephraim and successfully anchored in Horseshoe Island harbor, we were both ready for a big meal. I had even brought along champagne for the occasion.

When Kelly finally announced that she was going to make supper, I asked, "What are we having?" I imagined a tasty shrimp salad, then pasta and garlic bread.

"Poorboy sandwiches."

"Really," I said, barely masking my disappointment, having had my fill of cold cuts lately, which I had lived on for three days, in fact.

"I didn't know if you had electricity aboard. If we weren't at a marina, I mean." She stared at the two humongous rolls she'd brought.

"Got the standard-issue alcohol stove and enough of a gas generator to get us by, I suppose."

"Well . . . sorry." She really didn't look sorry, but more annoyed, and turned away and opened a cupboard to locate the plastic dinner plates.

"*Sorry?!*" I said. "Don't be sorry. I love poorboy sandwiches." Trying to make up quickly for my tactlessness.

"You better because you're gonna get your fill. Besides, I liked the poetic appropriateness of the entree. Since we are only teachers, right? *Unemployed* teachers."

By now she'd brought the plates to the counter and had set in motion her sandwich assembly line.

"And that brings up another question," I went on, "since appropriateness is the issue here."

"And that would be?"

"Which champagne goes best with hard salami?"

"We have a choice?" She looked at me, sounding cautious.

"I bought one each of the only brands I could find . . . afford. So it's either Kalifornia Splendor, at $9.95 a bottle, or Marsky's Bold Brut, which I feel I stole at $11.99."

"A bottle?"

"Yes, a bottle," I said, laughing. "Let me open the Marsky's first. It could be a real find, one of those beautiful things you acquire if you're lucky."

"Or it could be something a guy brewed up in his garage on a bet."

Again I chuckled. "Could be. I think it is local," I added, staring at the label. "Uh-huh, very local, in fact."

So I pulled the cork on the more expensive champagne and poured two glasses, then took a taster's sip of mine.

"Not bad, as far as I can tell."

"Are you an aficionado or just lucky?"

"You decide."

"Have champagne often, do you?" she teased, building our sandwiches.

"About as often as most unemployed teachers, I suppose."

Then Kelly stopped working and picked up her glass. "Cheers, Captain," she said, clinking hers with mine.

"To you. My first house guest."

We took tentative sips.

"You're right," Kelly said, sounding surprised. "It isn't that bad. It'll make these poorboys taste like porterhouse."

We sat down to sandwiches and champagne and when we were done, the sky had gone from deep blue to pink to mauve to dark purple. The seas were near calm. The big bottle of Marsky's Bold Brut was emptying quickly.

Feeling a nice buzz, about to drain the last drops from my glass, I stared across the dinette table at Kelly and commented, "You look lovely tonight, Ms. Shelberg. Would you care to step out on the aft deck for a dance in the moonlight?"

"There's no moon yet," she said, again sounding wary. "And I look just like you, remember?"

"Can we still check on the moon?"

"You really want to get me outside?"

"I feel like dancing."

She gave me a puzzled grin. "You're not drunk, right?" she asked with an unnervingly direct stare. "I don't want you falling overboard."

"Not a chance. I just want to celebrate."

"And what are we celebrating?"

I opened my mouth, but then stopped myself. What could I say? I certainly wasn't ready to give her details about my discoveries regarding Parnell, the writing he had left behind, or the guy who kept coming aboard *Siren Song* uninvited.

"Freedom," I finally answered.

"But there's more, right? Your mental wheels are visibly turning in *very* slow motion. Thanks to the Marsky's, I imagine."

"There's always more," I responded. "Dance?"

"We don't have any music."

"Says who?" I stood up, slowly and carefully, gripping the dinette table tightly, steadying myself, then stepped over to the nearby cabinet where I kept the battery-powered boom box and a few tapes. I popped in a favorite cassette, an old slow-jazz collection dominated by the haunting tones of a melancholy but sensual tenor sax. I set the volume just loud enough for us to get the beat.

Then I turned to Kelly, bowed slightly, extended my elbow, and said, "If you please, m'lady?"

"I believe I will, kind sir," she answered in a mock southern accent, standing, curtsying, and then following me out to the cockpit, where I took her in my arms. We began to sway rhythmically to the erotic riffs and runs of the instrumental.

"There's not a lot of room to make moves out here," Kelly said softly, so close to my ear.

"Just enough, I think."

"I meant dance steps."

"Me, too."

"Well, we're not moving much right now. What're we attempting?"

"The Marsky Champagne Shuffle."

She froze a moment, then gave a brief nervous laugh, holding herself close again and whispering, "I like you, I do. But isn't this an amazing act of trust?"

"What?" I wondered, sobering quickly at her tone.

"Going out on this boat, alone with you, a guy I barely know, away from anyone who could help me if you decided to get ideas."

"Don't worry. I've got 'moral character.' Somebody said that once, probably my mom."

"Very noble," she said. "Very admirable."

We danced.

Then she murmured, "But what if we *both* get ideas?"

That made me pull back far enough to find her staring up at me, her lips slightly parted, her pretty face aglow. The two of us weren't pretending to dance anymore. "Why then . . . of course . . . *naturally* . . ."

But before I could come up with any sort of nifty quip, Kelly took my face in her hands and brought herself fully to me, kissing me hard, passionately, on the mouth. And again. And again.

"There," she said, retreating a half-step. "That's done. Can we relax now? Just relax? I mean, the atmosphere is too goddam *charged*." She smiled.

"I don't see why not." I felt short of breath, dizzy. A sexy, charming young woman wanted me . . . right?

But instead of dancing, she wordlessly took my wrist and guided me back into the cabin.

I stopped her, gave her a last chance to change her mind. "We could try the Kalifornia Splendor," I suggested.

After staring at the deck for a moment, she lifted her eyes, fixed her gaze on me, took my right hand in both of hers, and said, "Forget it, Captain." Leading me to my mid-ship bunk.

When we awoke together the next morning, nestled comfortably in my cozy berth, a warm breeze wafting through the cabin, Kelly was the first to speak. She turned to me, placed her hand softly on my cheek, and stroked it delicately. We stared at one another until finally she said, "We're maybe playing this one a little over our heads, huh?"

She embraced me again, then said, "Know what I was thinking when I woke up?"

"What?"

"I was remembering one of the first mornings I spent in Door County. The air was so fresh, full of cedar and pine. I was at a church camp that summer. I must have been only nine or ten."

"Church camp, huh?" I said, tracing her face with my fingertips. "Is that where you got this?" Touching her scar. "Fighting with the boys?"

"That came later, in high school. And it is a battle wound."

"Oh yeah?"

"I got elbowed in a championship basketball game by a big girl with a real bad attitude. She kept calling me *princess bitch*, among other things."

"There must have been lots of blood," I remarked. "I've seen guys take hits like that fairly often."

"I soaked through a towel. They wanted to call an ambulance. But when my coach tried to sit me down, I said, 'NO! Tape it up and *bring it on*! I can't let her think she's whipped me.'"

"So you kept playing?"

"I went back in the game but there was no *playing*. I worked her over pretty good and we won. I think my teammates were impressed. I know the big girl was surprised."

"Tough customer."

"I don't fuck around," she said with quiet intensity, her blue eyes holding mine. "And I mean that in every way."

There was a two-beat pause between her last words and her next gentle squeeze. "But I like you a lot," she said. She kissed me, pulled back, bracing herself on an elbow, and stared at me again. "What I'm really wondering is why you hang around here."

"I'm cruising."

"But not seriously, right?"

"Seriously for me, at my skill level."

"What I mean is, are you going to *really* cruise? You know, cross the big water and take in Mackinac Island, Charlevoix, Traverse Bay?"

"I'm a *rookie* at this," I explained. "You gotta crawl before you can walk."

"There's not more to it?"

"My staying close to Door?"

"Uh-huh."

"There's you," I said. Making it simple. Maintaining the mask.

"That's not enough," she replied, taking me aback.

So I felt compelled to add: "Well, I guess there is a sort of project I'm working on. But it's still so speculative, so uncertain, it's hard to talk about."

Staring calmly at me, her expression momentarily un-
readable, Kelly said, "This non-conversation is getting too
weird." Pulling the sheet up under her chin.

"Just believe me, okay? Let me figure this out. That'll be
best."

"Believe you? When you won't confide in me at all, even
a hint." That wariness again.

"I can't."

"Can't or won't?"

"Please don't get mad."

"I'm not *mad*," she replied softly. "It's just . . . well, don't
you remember my telling you that I've done this routine
already? With Jimmy? Didn't I make that pretty clear?
Playing games and having secrets and making comments
that can't or won't be explained—that's all I got from
Jimmy and too many other people, and I really don't want
any more of it, ever."

I felt terrible, not only because I'd obviously hurt her,
but also because her tone was so tender, even despairing.

So I said, "Look, Kelly, I'm sorry. I am. I will come clean,
I promise."

"You're not very convincing," she said, with punishing
candor.

I took her in my arms again, risked pulling her steadily
to me, my hand at the small of her sleek back, cupping
her, fitting her into our embrace.

And she responded by slowly hooking her leg over
mine, her hand going to my hip.

Back in Sister Bay that noon, Kelly said she needed time
to rest up for the half-shift she was scheduled to work.

We'd eaten breakfast aboard *Siren Song*, and Kelly had been "dazzled" by my sparking/rocking-wave coffeemaker. Now, we walked silently to her car. The only words I could manage: "See ya, and soon, I hope."

She made no reply, only giving me a very guarded and tentative one-armed embrace, which she quickly stepped out of.

"What's wrong?" I asked. There was a close, palpable tension. My left hand went to my pants pocket and found the always present plastic ID badge among the business cards I'd been collecting. I began nervously flicking the ID card with the edge of my thumb.

"This wasn't a mistake, right?" she said, still hugging her beach bag. "Just another dumb thing I did?"

For the first time since I'd met her, the self-assurance that had characterized her every word and gesture suddenly wavered.

"It better not be," I answered, still rhythmically snapping the ID.

Then Kelly stared down at my pants pocket. "What's that noise?" she asked, distracted and irritated. "What are you *doing*?"

"Oh, it's just this," I answered, pulling out the photo ID and showing it to her. Kelly took it, glanced at it, and laughed.

"This looks like a mug shot," she said. "But hey, if it makes you feel any better, you're much nicer-looking in person." She handed back the card. "Just don't go popping it that way," she added. "You sound like a ticking bomb."

I put away the badge, looked up, and found Kelly smiling warmly once again.

"Soooo . . ." she said, shrugging and shuffling, "thanks for the cruise and the wonderful Marsky's Brut and *everything* it inspired. Oh, and don't forget."

I stared back, mystified.

"The hiders of this world must have a seeker," she announced, tossing her bag in the Civic's backseat, then climbing in and slamming her door, revving up the engine and accelerating down the highway in a trail of exhaust fumes.

And that's when I realized I'd forgotten to ask her for Nelson Brite's phone number. Or if Nelson Brite even had a phone number.

CHAPTER 13

So Kelly was gone, and by the afternoon I'd have to be gone, too. My slip was taken and no others had opened up. Something called *start of the season* negating my personal dockage needs. I did have to pick up some groceries, but I wouldn't be collecting much in the way of supplies since I had to walk at least a mile and hand-carry any purchases back to *Siren Song*. Adding to my list of irritations was talk that the weather might soon be changing for the worse. Bad news for a novice skipper with no idea of a safe harbor for the coming night, and with no confidence in his ability to properly set anchors in storm conditions.

Before gathering my supplies, I ducked into Al Johnson's looking for Nelson Brite. For once he wasn't there. Still, I walked through the restaurant, over to the counter where Brite usually sat. I spotted his usual waitress and asked her if Nelson Brite had a phone number.

"Not unless he tells you personally what it is," she said, picking up two plates piled high with lunch. I was about to back off, feeling shut out again, when she added, "Like Nelson always says, 'I don't want to talk to anyone I don't want to talk to.'"

"Makes sense," I said, in parting.

Later, with the afternoon slipping away, I crossed the small parking lot at the village dock, lugging what I hoped would be enough food. But even with a heavy grocery bag in either arm, I wasn't so preoccupied that I failed to notice the dented beige pickup truck sitting conspicuously alone at the far end of the asphalt apron. I thought: It couldn't possibly be, not the same truck that was trailing Parnell in the fog, for there was no hand-painted Packer insignia on the door, just as I remembered. Despite my misgivings, I continued very cautiously toward my boat, searching for silhouettes of thieves in the windows.

Finally, I stepped down into the cockpit, turning to set my groceries on the stern benchseat before digging in my pockets for the cabin key. But there was no need for that, I soon discovered. Because immediately after I leaned the bags against the seat back, I heard the cabin door open and the words "Pick 'em up and get the fuck in here."

I pivoted toward the voice coming from inside the cabin, and there he was again—the same wiry, twitchy little creep that I'd seen climbing around on *Siren Song* up in Pedersen Bay. I also noticed an ugly revolver in his right hand, pointed directly at me.

"You fuckin' *hear* me?!" the guy said a little louder, but not loud enough to draw attention to himself from others at the marina. "I said get the hell in here . . . *now!*"

"You mind if I put away the groceries?" I asked, pointing a thumb over my shoulder, trying hard to appear nonchalant.

"Didn't I just tell ya to bring 'em in? Too late now, asshole. Fuck your groceries. Won't need any groceries you don't get your ass in here, close the fuckin' door."

I did as ordered, leaving the two grocery bags in the cockpit. I entered the cabin, watching the creep back up a step to give me room, as he held the gun on me shakily. I wanted to think this guy was "Raymond Bruder" but I wasn't all that certain his voice was the same one I'd heard on the tapes. Twitching, surly, short-tempered, the creep meant business now. Sniffing like a cokehead, jerking his chin, shifting his eyes manically, the guy was wired. Again, there was the sickening smell of cigarette smoke. I spotted one of my coffee cups on the console being used as an ashtray.

"What's this all about?" I snapped, feeling reckless, my pocketed left hand breaking off a corner of the laminated faculty ID.

The little guy froze, then stared back unblinking, barely breathing, mouth hanging slightly open, seeming to notice me for the first time. The late afternoon sun was streaming in the side windows, and I could see that his longish dark hair flecked with gray was thinning, that his two-day growth of beard couldn't hide the acne scars of a rough adolescence. With his free hand he reached for the cigarette pack in his shirt pocket, shook out a smoke, pulled it away with his lips, replaced the pack, and lit up with a Bic disposable.

Finally he replied: "Start the fuckin' engine. The lines are free. We're goin' on a little cruise."

"Where?"

"Don't worry about *where*. Just start this fuckin' piece-a-shit!" he spat back. "Fuckin' Bayliner!" Added like a curse. "About all he deserved, fuckin' cop."

So I started up and backed away from my slip while he blew a stream of smoke at me.

"Get this scow over to Chambers Island," he said. "By the town park. Know where that is?"

I nodded.

"Then *move* it! We got us some work. Least you have. Tearing down this shit pile till I get what I came for."

As I brought *Siren Song* out of the harbor and pointed her west into Green Bay, I risked commenting, "What's to find? You already tossed the whole boat, twice I think."

He came back with "You playin' dumb now, asshole? Like you don't know whose boat this was?"

As he talked, I still couldn't say with certainty that his was the voice from the Q & A sessions. So I took another chance. I answered, "I know a cop owned it before me. Was he the one who was supposed to have those tapes you stole?"

That remark set his face seriously atwitch, his eyes squeezing shut, the tip of his cigarette flaring.

"You listen to 'em?" he asked.

"Uh-uh."

He decided to move behind me then, still holding the gun on me. He let the silence lengthen, the tension build. "You sure?" he asked, his sickening breath on my face. I was ready to attack just to get rid of the smell.

"Yeah, I'm sure," I answered.

"Find any more? Cuz there's gotta be more."

"No. *You* find any more?"

"Fuck would I be askin'? . . . Dumbshit."

Out ahead I noticed the sun was disappearing behind a line of dark clouds, and now I started to feel exposed on all fronts. Was it really only the night before that I was dancing on deck in the moonlight?

Then from my kidnapper I heard, "You know anything about that cop, that Parnell?"

"Only that this was his boat and he just died in a car accident." I turned my head to get a peek at the gunman, but he yelled, "Eyes front, asshole! Keep your fuckin' eyes on course!" Before turning away, I saw him reach inside his stained blue work shirt and give his chest a frantic scratching. Then just as quickly, he pulled his hand free and grabbed his crotch, adjusting his genitals. "You hear me!?" he shouted. "Eyes front!"

I obeyed.

He continued: "That cop had something of mine, something I been after for a long time."

"What is it you're after?" I asked finally. "Just tell me and get this over with. Because it's all a big mistake."

"Like I'm gonna talk, huh? And then maybe you get there first and cut me out?"

"Can't help you find anything if I don't know what we're looking for." I felt helpless. This wasn't anything like reprimanding some high school kid for muttering, "Aw, shit!" when he'd flunked a test or accidentally slammed his hand in a locker. But I wanted the guy to keep talking until I was absolutely sure one way or the other if his voice was on that tape. And he was starting to sound more familiar.

"I'll do the *finding*, asshole," he blared, calling me back to this nightmare. "Thing you'll do is demolition."

"But you're sure it's here, on the boat."

Before he responded, I observed big-bellied thunderheads already massing. The blackened sky soon looked low enough to touch.

"Trashed the guy's fuckin' apartment awhile back, but no luck. And he's got no safety deposit box nowhere."

"How do you know?"

"You think I'm fuckin' *stupid?* I got people who figure out shit like that. Know all about computers. Can find anything on anybody."

"I suppose."

"Fuckin' A! Then he moves aboard this shit-heap full-time. So I figure it's here somewhere."

"And worth all this hassle and trouble to have it, huh?"

"Bet your ass. He took it, and I'm takin' it back. Guy was a bad cop. You know that, right? Into some bad shit. For sure rippin' off the wrong people, dudes that always get even. So I'm absolutely A-one fuckin' positive he's holdin' it."

"Whatever *it* is."

"I'll get it, don't you worry. Even things up *totally.*"

"With Parnell?" Looking back at him.

He glared at me, said slowly: "Who the fuck else? Shit-head's been ridin' my ass for *years,* tryin' to stick me with all kindsa shit. Fuckin' conspiracy freak. He said that to me once. He goes, 'I'm a real conspiracy freak.' I said, 'No shit, Sherlock.' Then he slaps me upside the head. Fuckin' prick. But we kicked his ass, huh. Kicked it good. Holdin' out on me? No way, José! Dumb fuck."

I fell silent, stunned by his seeming admission of involvement. Had this guy been *that* pickup truck driver, the one trailing Parnell, maybe the first to rear-end him, push him out of control? The fatal collision with the semi had to have been pure chance, a genuine accident. But the pickup driver could certainly have set things in motion. And who's *we?* This creep and Kay Farrow?

"Hey listen," I started. "The weather's looking a little—"

"*Fuck* the weather, shithead! Weather won't matter, you don't tell me what I want to know." Dropping his cigarette near my feet, grinding it out, and shaking free another.

I felt the barrel tip of his snub .38 grazing against my head, just behind my left ear.

"Gonna have some serious brain damage, *you* hold out on me. Don't want to end up in the water like the cop, right?"

"Hold out *what?* I t-told you—I don't have any fuckin' idea what you're after, what the hell you're talking about. There's nothing aboard but stock equipment, just regular marine gear and supplies. So, lay off!"

"Don't know nothin', huh. And pokin' the guy's ex-wife, too."

That left me speechless and terrified. All I could think to say was "You mind bringing in those groceries before the rain starts?"

"*Fuck* your fuckin' groceries!! You gonna tell me or what?!"

By this time, the first swollen raindrops had begun to fall, pinging and snapping against the deck of the command bridge, as I rounded the north side of Chambers Island.

"Then let me get 'em. You might want to eat sometime, too."

And just that quickly the coming storm organized itself, sending winds whipping over the water, raising whitecaps, rocking the boat.

"C'mon, man," I pleaded. "Just let me get my stuff inside. Paid good money for it."

"Oh yeah? Whose money?"

"What?" I replied, just as the first explosion of thunder shook the cabin.

"Aw, fuck," he said, conceding. Then, "Move it, *haul ass!*" And he grabbed a fistful of my shirtsleeve and pulled me from the pilot's chair, shoving me toward the cabin door. By now the swells were building so rapidly that I could see the bags of groceries starting to bounce and slide across the aft bench. In another few seconds they'd be water-soaked, then airborne, then breaking open all over the deck.

"I'll hurry," I said, pushing open the cabin door and striding aft, stumbling, reaching for the grocery bags, grabbing them both just before a big swell slammed into the starboard bow, shaking the whole vessel, forcing me to plant my feet like a boxer fighting for balance after getting tagged a good one. A quick look all around through the slashing rain and howling wind revealed a gathering of dangerously large swells coming at us. No other watercraft were visible in any direction.

Pivotal Moment for JP Griffin. I could see a genuine McGee maneuver taking shape. I took another step toward the cabin and hollered, "Hey, get the door!" By now the wet paper bags were about to disintegrate in my hands and spill the contents all around the cockpit.

He pushed open the door and as he leaned into it, I charged him, smashing the sodden grocery bags into his face, bouncing his head off the doorjamb, knocking loose the gun that went skittering across the aft deck. He surprised me by shoving back and making a dive for the gun. I took a wild swing at his head as he reeled by, a glancing blow but enough to knock him off balance and drop him to the cockpit deck. Cans of vegetables, soup, tuna, and boxes of cereal, pasta, and crackers were scattered everywhere, and he fell right into the center of the mess. The goddam little pisspot rolled over and grabbed a can of soup. He aimed it at my head, but the heaving of *Siren Song* caused the can to arc harmlessly overboard. I couldn't help but notice it was Campbell's Select: Chicken with Egg Noodles, my favorite.

The gun had slid to the far corner of the aft deck, and the intruder lurched madly to retrieve it. I dove on top of him, driving my knee into his back, pulling his left arm behind him, jerking it into a hammerlock, ready to break his shoulder. I was imitating the action stars, not having been in a fight since fifth grade. My moves seemed to work. Caught in my grip, the creep went momentarily slack, lifeless.

Still pinning him hard against the garbage-filled deck, I tried to dig out his wallet, just like cops did to perps in the movies, wanting to know who the hell he was, where he lived, what he did for work. But I wasn't as efficient as movie cops. I felt the top edge of a billfold in his back pocket but couldn't get a grip. Then I pushed at the pocket bottom and the wallet fell out.

Before I could grab it, he erupted with another surprising display of adrenaline-hyped willpower, pushed himself to all fours, rolled me off him, took a sweeping backhanded swing, and clipped me across my forehead. Again he went for the gun. But just as he palmed the .38, a split second before he could stand and square himself for a good shot at me, *Siren Song* took a direct hit from an oncoming five-foot wall of water, the deck engulfed, the boat heeling dangerously. The gunman hurled right past me and over the port side. He never even screamed as I watched him disappear under the crest of another big breaker. By now the storm had shoved us well beyond Chambers Island.

I held on for dear life to the topside ladder, struggling to pull myself back inside the cabin as *Siren Song* regained her trim. Then, inpulsively, swearing at myself for doing so, I grabbed the old-style decorative/accessory life preserver hanging starboard of the cabin door, and heaved the *Siren Song* ring in my attacker's direction. I saw the life ring splash down and float off, and I swore at myself again, realizing I'd just left a calling card at the scene of the crime.

Suddenly, another rogue wave slammed over the gunwale and filled the cockpit, flooding the cabin just as I was able to haul myself back through the doorway. I pulled the cabin door shut and jumped to the controls, hurrying to right the vessel. That's when I remembered a relevant and very crucial bit of Kriel advice: "Always *heave to*—head into the weather—with the weather on your port-side bow." Terrified, I attempted the maneuver and steadied *Siren Song* while praying for a break in the squall. If I could just somehow run south-southeast, I thought, I could get away from the path of the stormline.

For a brief moment, I considered coming about and searching for the man overboard. I didn't want his death on my hands. But his staying alive meant I would always be in jeopardy. Still, I'd never done anything like this my entire adult life—fight, kill. I hated how I felt. Yet I left him and angled away from the storm, finally throttling up and cutting over to race toward calmer waters. The engine didn't sound good, though. Something important must have been jarred loose by the rogue wave.

As I struggled to hold my course, I remembered the intruder's wallet. It had slid aside on the aft deck as he lunged at me. Probably washed overboard, along with the little creep and most of my groceries. I looked down at my hands on the wheel. They were shaking. So was the rest of me. I was soaked through and the wind was still howling.

Siren Song had begun to make noises I'd never heard before, and the engine seemed to be losing power little by little. I knew I needed to limp back to port somehow, somewhere, anywhere other than Sister Bay. Thank God the waves and wind seemed to be diminishing.

By now it was completely dark. I could see no lights visible in any direction. I felt sure *Siren Song* had circled back around Chambers Island after our tussle, so I set a course that would take me down to Egg Harbor. Much sooner than I expected, I found myself coming out of the wind and rain and high seas and closing in on Egg Harbor under more favorable conditions. I needed to get out of my wet clothes. I needed to get *Siren Song* cleaned up, dried out, repaired. There was, I knew, serious damage. I'd begun to smell strange odors emanating from below. Running away by boat didn't sound like an option anymore.

CHAPTER 14

I was lucky, luckier than I deserved. First, I found a rare open slip in Egg Harbor, though it took nerve to make myself put in there. My instincts told me to keep going, even if I had to abandon *Siren Song* and grab somebody else's boat. I would race down to Green Bay, the Fox River, pressing on until I ran out of gas or navigable water, then find some other means of transportation to take myself as far away from Door County as fast as possible.

My other lucky find: Wedged beneath two heavy, soaked-through boxes of breakfast cereal, the wallet had been pinned back in the starboard corner of the cockpit. A hand-tooled cordovan leather billfold, it contained damn little information about its owner, but it did reveal my tormentor's full name. Raymond Sloan Rudert. *Sloan.* What, a nephew? Grandson maybe? And I didn't have to challenge my imagination much to surmise what he'd come looking for. The guy truly believed in The Money. That it was real, that it still existed, and that I had it aboard whether I realized it or not.

But that last name: Rudert . . . Rudert. Hadn't the narrator on the tapes clearly said *Bruder*? That's what I'd heard anyway. But the names were similar in sound. Maybe Parnell had mixed the names for the taping. Disguised them for some reason, if that had actually been Parnell talking. In the wallet the only other contents were twenty-two dollars in cash and a business card for MAXIM COMMUNICATIONS. And the name of the associate listed on the card? Shay Farrell.

That was one business card I didn't dare pocket. I put it right back where I found it, thinking: Shay Farrell, *Kay Farrow*. Another two-name sound-alike. Could she have been the woman Parnell had interviewed? Was she the other young woman in Parnell's story, the one who tried to seduce/swindle Sloan out of his money, only to have Parnell snatch it up at the end of the Northport dock? Did I want to meet her, too? Uh-uh, not at all. It was definitely time to run again, pull out and disappear, hope for better circumstances elsewhere, almost anywhere.

But first I had to know what the world knew, if anything, about what I'd just survived, what I'd just done. I wanted to find the next day's newspaper, listen to the local radio and TV news, learn if any drownings had been reported, any missing persons listed, anything specific that might make our stormy confrontation a public issue, an incident deserving aggressive scrutiny by local law enforcement. I had to know if I'd let a man die out there. So I had to make myself sit tight on *Siren Song* for a while. I knew I couldn't stay here, though, in Egg Harbor. I felt too confined, trapped. So I considered risking the short cruise back to Sturgeon Bay, where I could get *Siren Song* repaired and check on my Jeep, make sure it was ready for a hasty departure, a sudden escape.

Again I heard my conscience saying: Why don't you simply go to the police for help and protection? Tell them all you know and let them do the job they're paid to do? But by now I didn't dare trust them because all I could think about was Rudert's offhand evaluation of Parnell: "Guy was a bad cop. You know that, right? Into some bad shit" is what the little weasel had said. Go to the police? No thanks. If there was one bad cop, chances were there were more. Unless Rudert was dead wrong.

That night, with my windows latched and cabin door both locked and roped shut from the inside, with all the shades and curtains drawn and the galley lights dim, I tried to calm myself with warm tomato soup and three plastic-wrapped dinner rolls, the only salvageable groceries. I hoped for a few hours of fitful sleep. With the engine off, the bad air inside wasn't so irritating.

But sleep wouldn't come. So I got up and grabbed the very last of the JDM/McGee novels. After I crawled back in my berth and got comfortably adjusted, I opened the paperback and found two 3 × 5 cards inside the novel, placed nearly in the middle of the book, next to a page containing the only underlining I had found in any of the mysteries. I read the cards first. The one on top was simply an address in Pensacola, Florida, with no name listed. The other card was a note, a two-line message that took my breath away and set my tired, straining heart racing. Because on the second card Parnell, I assume, had typed:

EKC—
Listen carefully to the talk.
S was going to die anyway (and I can prove it).
Put bonus jack in boat (N/UP)

"Put bonus jack in boat"? What the hell did that mean? I wondered, sitting up straight now, holding my head, trying to steady myself—*jack*, with a lowercase "j." A *car* jack? Boats like *Siren Song* don't need jacks. Their trailers do, but who was going to be trailering a craft as big and heavy as my Bayliner? Not me. Not Parnell. *Jack* had other nautical meanings, though. It could refer to ship flags or masthead supports or even certain kinds of fish.

Then I heard a line echoing in my head, a snip of dialogue from the required reading list in American Lit, Steinbeck's *Of Mice and Men*. It had to have been George who talked about sitting in some barroom "blowin' our jack."

Jack . . . cash . . . *The Money.*

Then I thought: My God, was this the cover note that should have gone to EC with the cassette tape, but for some reason didn't?

Next, I looked at the underlined passage in the McGee mystery. The focus excerpt described an aluminum box with a rubber waterproof gasket, where McGee kept his emergency cash. And McGee usually kept this box hidden in the bilge of his houseboat, tucked in a space below the waterline.

I finished reading, absolutely convinced Parnell was the "boy" at the Sloan death scene that stormy December night twenty years earlier. Parnell had the man's typewriter, Parnell had all sorts of detailed inside information, and now it appeared that Parnell had The Money. Apparently, the cash that Parnell had taken from the Northport dock he'd *put in the boat* not merely in the sense of using it to purchase the vessel, but *put in the boat* meaning *Siren Song*. My vessel appeared to be the final hiding place for the balance of Sloan's wealth. So Rudert was right. But how did he know that? How did he know that Parnell would lead him to The Money? That Parnell had had it all along? And what the hell was "N/UP"? Now, at least, I knew where to begin looking.

I gathered up a small prybar, pliers, and flashlight from the bigger/better tool kit. Next, I untethered the cabin door. Then I stopped, frozen in place, as I tried to visualize what I'd do next. What if I were being watched? What if someone were waiting outside right now? I gripped the prybar firmly and eased open the cabin door, peeked outside, saw no one.

Crouching, staying out of sight, crawling along on the deck, I reached the engine hatch and pulled it open. I dropped down into the bilge section containing not just the engine but seemingly all the other gut-mechanicals necessary to make the boat run. It was a cramped fit. Down on all fours, I felt my knees and hands get slippery wet. It smelled like mildew, sulphur, oil.

I scanned the area with my light beam, squeezing myself deep into the bilge, and there, tucked away, bolted high against the port bulkhead, was another box marked NEW/USED PARTS, only this one, maybe a foot square and deep, was made of dark gray metal, locked, and waterproof. If Rudert had thoroughly searched the boat, how could he have missed noticing this container? Maybe he was a landlubber who didn't know a bilge could contain secrets. Maybe the box looked unremarkable.

Using the prybar, I snapped off a small padlock, popped the box open, pulled away a black plastic cover plate. And there it was, just as Parnell had hinted—rolls and rolls of bills, cash. Yes, I had found it, The Money! Fitted snugly into tightly sealed baggies.

I nearly reached out to take greedy handfuls but stopped myself with the thought of . . . *fingerprints*. Once I had touched The Money, once I had left my mark on the lost loot, I would then become just another link in the chain of crimes that dropped the money into my lap, a chain reaching all the way back to an unfortunate old farmer named Sloan. I needed a plan. I wondered: What would McGee do in this situation?

Then I remembered the surgical gloves. Again doing the army crawl, I returned to the cabin and hurried to the forward storage bins and the larger tool kit. There, still tucked against the side of the case, were the two pairs of latex gloves. I took out both pairs, pocketed one set and pulled on the other, then returned to the engine hatch. On my way through the galley, I grabbed a plastic bag I'd saved from my grocery shopping.

Once I'd gotten myself repositioned in the engine hold and had balanced the flashlight on some nearby conduit so that the beam shone squarely on The Money, I began to methodically, carefully, reverently place the weighty baggies of rolled bills into the larger plastic bag. When I had finished the transfer, I replaced the black plate and the NEW/USED PARTS box cover and tapped on it until it snapped shut. Though the padlock was broken, it still looked functional when fitted back in place.

I decided to count the cash in the head with the door locked and lights off. Full-blown paranoia had returned big time. Again relying solely on the flashlight beam for illumination, I initiated a slow and precise tallying of the "bonus jack" that Parnell had stowed away so cleverly and carefully. Two meticulous and complete countings later, I had to accept the fact that I was now the guardian of $494,650.00, mainly in hundreds, with a few fifties and 281 *thousand-dollar* bills thrown in. Nearly *ten years'* worth of veteran teacher pay! And there seemed to be nothing suspicious about the currency—no sequential serial numbers, no blue-dot markings on the corners, nothing I'd ever read about or seen in movies to indicate the money had an official banking or law enforcement past.

My hands still protected by the surgical gloves, I rubberbanded the cash into tight bricks according to denomination. Then I placed the seven bricks into a brown paper grocery sack, taping that securely closed. I planned to hide The Money in a gym bag that I could inconspicuously transport to my Jeep. If I had to, I would then put it all in a safe deposit box at some area bank.

It crossed my mind that I should try to remove ASAP the false-bottomed box containing the McGee books (and all of Parnell's damning documents), as well as the Smith Corona portable typewriter (which hid my own incriminating notes). All were buried deep in the V-berth storage bins. That maneuver would have to be carefully executed for me to avoid notice. I didn't want anybody asking why I was moving off *Siren Song*. And if I decided to take The Money and run—an impulse that was, I'm embarrassed to say, quickly becoming Option One—I needed to work out a plausible explanation for leaving the area. Surely Kriel would request credible reasons for my shortened cruise. I had only been out two weeks.

But as I stuffed The Money into my black Nike gym bag, covering the package with sweatsocks and running shoes, I recalled another suddenly relevant detail from one of Parnell's newspaper clippings on Sloan. Quickly, I retrieved the book box, emptied the JDM paperbacks onto my bed and pulled the appropriate envelope from the secret compartment. And there it was, the claim that Sloan "might very well have been carrying as much as $100,000 to $150,000 when he left his home for the last time."

That meant Parnell had either acquired a bonanza far exceeding the newspaper's low-ball estimate of Sloan's holdings *or* Parnell had invested the original funds most wisely and profitably *or* Parnell had stashed with the Sloan money a ton of payola from his own schemes (the "bad shit" and "rip-offs" Rudert had referred to). All those possibilities made my situation more and more dangerous, my vulnerability more and more acute. What if Parnell's former police colleagues were looking into his activities? What if Parnell was part of some rogue cop contingent, some in-house extortion ring?

Strangely, though, my next thought—after realizing I was now, if only temporarily, a very rich, unemployed civil servant—focused on Kelly Shelberg. She certainly deserved a cut of the take, a very major cut. I mean, Parnell had clearly held out on her, hardly lavished her with a generous divorce settlement. She had a legitimate claim to his assets. But I could only disburse funds if I dared to simply keep all the cash. Which at the moment seemed like the path of least resistance and least personal risk. Because if I ever attempted to return The Money, I would not only bring the glare of publicity on pasts that many people would likely want to remain hidden, but on myself as well. Wouldn't I have a helluva lot of explaining to do? Hadn't I withheld evidence that could easily be argued was central to solving an ongoing criminal investigation?

I felt I was getting too clever and slick for my own good. I had now reached the point in my rationalizing where *doing the right thing*—giving up money that wasn't mine—would not only be dangerous but stupid. Quickly, I took the opposite tack. It really wasn't anybody else's money either, as far as I could see, *unless* I counted the original $150,000 high estimate of Sloan's cash to be in dispute.

Perhaps I should talk to somebody about this. I needed perspective. I needed to find Kelly.

In truth, I was bowled over by the sudden possibility of having enough money to fund an extended period of untroubled free time, a period of focused contemplation that could result in my finding a new direction in life, or perhaps recommitting myself to a profession that I both loved and hated. Then, naturally, the image of Rudert intruded into my fantasy, bringing with it the certainty that trouble for me would always be close at hand. I didn't know if he was alive or dead. I had to be certain of his fate before I could even dare think about fleeing with the cash or conspiring with Kelly to split the proceeds. I was working on decisions that just a few days ago would have been unfathomable.

My troubled imaginings were interrupted by the onset of more annoying fumes from belowdecks. I was compelled to ease open two side windows to ventilate the cabin. I had no idea what was causing the noxious odor. It didn't smell like gas or oil but I couldn't be sure. A mixture of both and something else? Maybe Parnell had left a cracked container of some unstable chemical aboard, and the storm tossing agitated or spilled the substance.

I decided that first thing in the morning I would try to coax *Siren Song* back to Kriel's marina for repairs. Then, after I felt certain that nobody was paying any attention to me, I'd bring my Jeep to the dock area near my slip and off-load all of my incriminating new possessions—the book box, the typewriter, the gym bag that was going to make me rich.

CHAPTER 15

At 8:06 a.m. I was nosing *Siren Song* into an open slip close to Kriel's office building. The last mile of my short morning cruise sounded like it could be the last one ever for my vessel. The coughing and clanging vibrations coming from the power system belowdecks had me feeling certain I would soon burn out a bearing or blow a piston, some sort of terminal mechanical mishap. From Egg Harbor, I had called ahead to alert Kriel and got his voicemail. I probably should have called for a tow.

The slip I had selected seemed unmarked, yet for all I knew it could have been privately leased or reserved for boats Kriel was buying, showing, selling. But I had no choice. Then, just before I was able to shut down the engine, I heard a new sound, a keening wail ending in a high whine.

By the time I'd killed the power and tied up and retrieved the gym bag of cash, the noxious smell was building again at an alarming rate. So I locked down the vessel and, carrying the Nike duffel, climbed onto the finger pier. I planned first to hide The Money in my Wrangler, then go back for the book box and typewriter, if the coast was clear. Once those were stowed, I would seek out Kriel for a diagnosis on *Siren Song.* But Kriel found me first.

"Got your message," he began, squinting at my boat, as if he couldn't believe something major had gone wrong with a Kriel Deal. "Didn't hit anything, didja?"

"It hit me," I said.

"What hit you?"

"A big wave. A couple, actually."

"Yesterday? You were out in that blow?"

"Not long. It came up so fast."

"Learn you a lesson, I hope. If a storm's comin' from across the bay, it'll get here quick. Damn things always arrive sooner than expected. Now, describe the trouble."

So I ran through my repertoire of imitative sounds in the sequence that I remembered hearing them. All the while Kriel looked increasingly, uncharacteristically grim.

"You have any guests aboard recently?" he asked.

"Yeah, one." I should have explained all and asked for Kriel's advice. Instead, I kept my mouth shut.

"Not somebody who'd fool with anything, I hope."

How could I answer that? Say: Yeah, Wally, yesterday there was this guy who came aboard uninvited to fool with *me.* But he got bounced *over*board in the storm. And then I took off on him, taught *him* a lesson.

"I don't think so," I hedged. "Why? Does it sound bad?"

"Doesn't sound good. We can't tell anything for sure till we get in there and snoop. Can you leave it for a while?"

"Uh-huh. Can't go anywhere with it now. I've got a few errands that'll take some driving around. So be my guest." Gesturing at my crippled cruiser.

"I'll try and free up one of the guys by afternoon, get you a worst-case scenario."

"Don't be so optimistic," I kidded, gripping the handle on the gym bag even tighter, seeing that I couldn't very well go back aboard and retrieve the book box and typewriter as I'd intended, not without arousing interest or even suspicion from Wally Kriel.

"Who knows, you may get lucky," offered Kriel. "Let's hope, huh?"

So I handed Wally the keys to *Siren Song* and walked off toward the parking lot and the Jeep I hadn't seen in over two weeks. On finding it, I walked around it carefully. Had it been violated or damaged or sabotaged or destroyed by Rudert? For once my paranoid fears were unfounded. The modest, faded blue Wrangler was right where I'd left it—locked, unlooted, all four tires still holding air. I climbed in and fired up the engine, then started toward Sister Bay.

While driving between Fish Creek and Ephraim, thinking mostly about Sister Bay, I rehashed my conversation with Kriel. I couldn't recall that I'd mentioned the smell in *Siren Song*, just the noisy clanging. And the more I thought about that smell the less sure I was that I'd left any windows open. I had become so used to closing the boat up tight anytime I would be away from it, that I'd probably stuck to my obsessive routine. But I couldn't turn back now. In Sister Bay, I could call Kriel from Al Johnson's.

First, though, I wanted to answer the question: What was the license plate number on that dented beige pickup in the marina parking lot? The truck that resembled the vehicle shadowing Parnell the night of his death, the one without a Packers logo? Unfortunately, that query would remain unresolved because when I slowly passed by the lot, the pickup was gone! This development left me more shaken, inspired me to consider unthinkable possibilities.

I turned off on the first side street past the marina, headed inland and looked for a place to pull over and park. My breathing was strained, my imaginings nightmarish. How could Rudert have managed to escape the storm? He hadn't looked like a strong swimmer to me. Only two possibilities presented themselves: 1) Rudert truly had *backup*, a partner to cover his ass, clean up his messes, move his truck, or 2) the truck wasn't actually Rudert's, had nothing whatever to do with him. Maybe Rudert *had* survived. Maybe somebody had fished him out of the bay, or he'd found my life ring and floated to Chambers Island. Or, who knows, maybe he did swim all the way back to the marina and driven the truck away himself.

I spent the next fifteen minutes replaying in my mind the boat-jacking, storm-and-fight scene, and lucky getaway. What if someone had observed Rudert going aboard *Siren Song*? What if someone had been watching when we left the marina and headed into stormy weather like a couple of idiots? Someone on the lake or shoreline tracking us with binoculars out of curiosity—as many of the coastline landowners are wont to do on lazy summer afternoons—and witnessed an incident they thought suspicious, incriminating, worth reporting. A few minutes was all it took to convince me I was still at risk. I had to get The Money stashed and get rid of Rudert's wallet *pronto*. I had to be *clean* of this dirty business.

But against my own instincts, what I did next was seek out Kelly Shelberg. I wanted to talk to her, confront her

with my other big question: Did she want us to be together, however temporarily, or what? So I started up the
Wrangler, drove onto the empty street, U-turned, and
headed back to Bay Shore Drive where I aimed for Al
Johnson's.

I parked on the main street and locked up the Jeep,
feeling for the cash-filled gym bag before climbing out of
the car. The Money was buried behind the passenger's
seat and covered with a blanket and box of CDs.

Walking once more into the always teeming lobby at
Al's, I didn't bother waiting for the hostess to acknowl-
edge me and offer help, but instead worked my way
through yet another boisterous breakfast crowd, scanning
the restaurant for Kelly. I had nearly crossed the entire
main floor and was closing in on the lunch counter at the
far end of the room when I heard a voice beside me say,
"She's off this morning."

Startled, I turned too quickly and found Nelson Brite at
my shoulder. His handlebar mustache twitched. He was
wearing a maroon sweatshirt and baggy blue jeans.

"Well, hello," I managed. Then, making one more vi-
sual sweep of the crowd, I asked, "Will she be coming in
sometime?"

"She said if you showed up to give you a number where
she can be reached." He handed me a folded slip of paper.

"Thanks." I looked at the note. It wasn't the unlisted
number Kelly had already given me.

"We all watch out for the special ones," he said, winking.

"She told me you know this scene best."

"I hang around, talk to people, see things."

"Then you write very well about what you've seen."

He laughed through his nostrils at that, twitched his
drooping mustache. "I try."

"You succeed. Especially profiling those old-timers. They really come to life."

"So you've read some of my stuff."

"Two books so far. Some gutsy criticism in both. Like naming the spoilers here, when you have to live with them. Finding tough stories worth telling." I was wondering how to bring up Parnell and his writing.

"You get what you need if you stay where you belong," he replied. "You also can get what you deserve. You want some coffee?" he asked, gesturing toward the lunch counter where his regular stool and the one next to it were open.

"Should I introduce myself?"

"You're JP, right?"

"Uh-huh."

"Nelson," he said, extending his hand. We shook and sat down.

Then Brite merely made eye contact with the waitress working the counter and instantly we had steaming mugs of fresh coffee in front of us.

"Telepathic communication," I observed, nodding at the waitress.

"The best kind." He blew on the coffee and took a sip. "You don't want to talk books, though."

"Writing actually." Finding my opening.

"Not the lovely Ms. Shelberg?"

"You know her pretty well?" I asked. I took too big a swallow of coffee and set my mouth aflame. Then I flashed back to the embrace Kelly and Brite had shared the last time we'd all been at Al's.

He didn't answer my question, but asked one of his own: "You know her ex did some writing?"

Telepathic communication.

"I did see his name in your writer's workshop essay." Trying to move carefully.

"Attended my fiction seminar a couple summers ago. Had a bunch of short stories. Cop stuff mostly. But not just gunfights and car chases. I remember one he called 'Pacing the Cage.' About how a prisoner organized and reorganized his cell so it would reflect his conscience, the state of his soul. Pretty impressive. Memorable."

"So he finished a class with you?"

"Nah. He wasn't much of a joiner, what you teachers today call a 'cooperative learner.' More a lone wolf. He had a lively mind and a thick accordion folder of manuscripts. I read a few of them, parts of others. Enough to tell he had talent."

Had Brite ever read the last part of "Champagne Shuffle"? Did Parnell ever submit the whole manuscript? How to find out? I tried: "Did he write only about Door County?"

"Mostly. You remember his 'starting points' approach— begin with some actual incident, then fictionalize a resolution for it."

I nodded, then recklessly asked, "Did he ever show you a story called 'Champagne Shuffle'? I found some notes about it."

Brite stared at me a second too long before slowly shaking his head. "What's it about?"

"Some old farmer." I stopped myself.

"Who drove off the Northport dock," said Brite. "The Sloan case."

I shrugged. "Maybe."

"Because he did mention wanting to write about that. Promised me a book proposal on it, in fact. Never delivered. Maybe dropped off an intro, I think. But he did send over a treatment for a novel he called *The Ass-Whipping Club*. Great title, huh? About a sort of rogue/vigilante cop character."

"Based on firsthand experience?"

Brite laughed again. "Jimmy was working lots of angles." He nodded to himself, staring at his placemat.

"Like what? You mean in his writing?"

Brite shook his head, glancing at me. "After-hours security," he clarified. "He helped out a bank vice-president buddy of mine in Sturgeon Bay. Shit, was that a mess."

"Can you say anything about it?"

"Only that it had to do with this guy's daughter. Scaring off some scumbag boyfriend." Bright looked away again, studied the dining room this time. "What I heard, anyhow," he concluded, bringing his gaze back. "Legitimate work, I guess, but close to the line, huh?"

"Did Kelly know about his writing or moonlighting?"

"Beats me. They were divorced a while before he came in for advice."

"Did you keep anything of his?"

Brite scowled briefly. "You gonna take up the cause?" he asked, his voice full of skepticism, suspicion. "Finish something he started?"

"I don't think so."

"Best to leave all that alone."

"All what?"

"Jimmy's other life."

Stunned, I paused just a moment before daring to say: "There's somebody else we both might know."

"Who's that?"

"Ever heard of a guy named Rudert? Ray Rudert?"

Brite frowned again. "A punk, an aging punk. A *repeat offender*. What's he to you, if you don't mind my asking?"

"His name was written on a notepad I found in the storage cabinet next to my berth on *Siren Song*." Feeling I'd already said too much.

Brite seemed to be contemplating my own facial expressions. "All I can think of, the only connection is Kriel."

"Wally Kriel?"

"The one and only."

"What connection?" My heart raced, fueled by caffeine and fright.

Instead of answering, Brite signalled the waitress, and again without a word being exchanged, she brought him a fresh blueberry muffin.

"Rudert works for Kriel," Brite continued. "At least he has recently."

"At the marina?"

"Sure. Where else?"

"Doing what?"

"Low-level stuff. Cleaning, detailing, some mechanical maintenance as he learns it, I suppose." Brite showed me a mischievous smile.

Detailing, I thought. So Rudert did steal the tapes.

"Kriel's not worried about Rudert's past?"

"Wally's greatest virtue and most glaring weakness is that he can't give up on people," Brite declared. "One rare bird."

I fell silent, staring at the floor, trying to take in the implications of this news. No wonder Rudert could come and go as he pleased on *Siren Song*. He must have had a master key or a duplicate of mine, being trusted in Kriel's world. But was Kriel to be trusted in mine?

I looked back at Brite and asked, "What are you working on now?" Going safely mundane again.

"The same novel I've been working on for the last ten years." He turned a somber face toward his half-eaten muffin.

"Ten *years*," Brite repeated more to himself than me, shaking his head.

"It'll happen," I said, standing, struggling for balance, reaching for my wallet to pay for coffee.

"Forget it," said Brite. "On me. In appreciation for your being a reader."

"You'll finish."

"I believe I will, yes. And I hope you do, too."

"Me? Finish what?"

"Your trip. Your quest. Kelly said you were cruising."

I nodded. "Well, thanks for the concern. And thanks for all this." I gestured expansively to take in Door County.

"Not mine to give, but it is yours to take," he responded, adding more mystery to a conversation that provided few definitive answers.

It wasn't till I was back on the road that I realized I'd also forgotten to ask Brite about his phone number.

CHAPTER 16

From the first phone booth I found, I called the new number Brite had given me for Kelly. She answered on the fourth ring. Her voice echoed as if she were in an empty room.

"You on a cell phone?" I asked.

"Econoline special. I know the sound is crappy."

"Just good enough," I said, glancing up and down Bay Shore Drive at the streams of tourists wandering along the walkways, the slow-and-go traffic clogging the road. I felt exposed. I felt *watched*. Then I realized I couldn't see my Jeep with its half a mil in unmarked currency. An RV/motorhome had parked between me and my Wrangler, blocking my view completely. Sweating now, I needed to find out quickly why I was calling Kelly—what did she have to tell me?

"Listen," she continued, "I need to see you, talk to you in person . . . right away. It's really important. I have to clear up some things, tie up lots of loose ends."

"Doesn't sound like an invitation to party." Sweat trickling down my ribs.

"No." Her mood and tone were somber, dead serious.

"Where are you now?" I asked.

"Peninsula State Park. Drive in at the north entrance and go to the Eagle Bluff lookout. I'll be in the parking lot."

"Right now?"

"Yes."

"I'm on my way." And we both hung up without saying goodbye. I cautiously approached my Wrangler, deemed it undisturbed, and climbed aboard.

In a little less than fifteen minutes, I had entered the expansive state park, the most popular of them all, 3,776 acres of wonderful wilderness, a peninsula on a peninsula, that no doubt had the real estate developers drooling with envy year after year. But year after year this gorgeous stretch of sandy beach and timbered hills, bold bluffs, and dazzling sunsets has been preserved for posterity by conscientious administrators. Thanks to them, the camping public would always have a chance to escape the drudgery and complexity of adulthood to lead a simpler life close to the earth. With Parnell's cash, I could live such a life *permanently*.

I found the Eagle Bluff parking lot and steered my Wrangler into a spot facing the smooth, glittering waters of Green Bay. Kelly sat inside her rusty Civic at the other end of the lot, which was fairly crowded. She got out, locked her door, and walked slowly over to the Jeep. I pushed open my passenger door for her, and she eased it back further.

She wore a baby-blue boatneck jersey, white shorts, running shoes. She looked so tan and fresh and vital, so *summer*. Yet, she seemed troubled. Even her smile was guarded, showing just a glimpse of her perfect teeth as she bit her lower lip. I was anxious for her to get in and close the door, maybe lock up. Just in case Rudert and his henchmen were behind some nearby tree, all wielding hatchets.

"You found it," she said, placing her right foot on the step, leaning in but not climbing aboard, not trusting herself to enter my space.

"Have a seat," I joked, patting the upholstery next to me. "Take a load off." Wondering what the vague pronoun "it" referred to. "Why are we meeting here?"

"I wanted us to see the place where we shared something I thought was pretty special. And I wanted to feel safe."

I looked out my windshield and down across the water 180 feet below us and there, maybe a mile off, almost within swimming distance, lay Horseshoe Island and the cove where Kelly and I spent our night together.

Still holding her tentative stance in the open doorway, Kelly took a deep breath and blurted, "I was in on it, okay?"

"In on what?" My breath thinning, sweat dripping and sliding again, my forehead greasy and slick.

"That guy who broke into your boat? He's a local named Rudert."

"I know."

Now it was Kelly's turn to go slack-jawed. "You do?" she replied. "How?"

"You first. Tell me everything." I took hold of her wrist and drew her slowly into the Jeep. She didn't protest.

"Well . . . I was *in on it*. But I didn't *know*, all right?" she contended, pulling the door closed. "I mean, they *used* me, and I didn't understand what they were going to do, were willing to do, until things got way out of hand."

"*They?*"

"Rudert mainly. But he said he had help." She was staring straight out the windshield, at Horseshoe Island, not me. I willed her to face me, but she wouldn't.

"Used you *how* exactly?" I was struggling to stay cool, focused.

"The day we first met, remember? That first time you ate at Al's. Right after you left the restaurant, Rudert showed. I'd never seen him before. He must have been following you. He caught me when I went on break and told me I was due a great deal of money, money my ex-husband had been hiding from me for years. I asked, 'What money?' and he said it was money Jimmy had stolen. But it was untraceable money, he said. All cash. And we both had a 'first-level interest' in recovering it. That's how he talked, like he was a bounty hunter."

I felt my stomach begin to churn. "Go on," I insisted, thinking her whole speech sounded rehearsed.

"He said if he could recover the money with my help, we'd split it. When I asked how much money he was talking about, he said maybe *$150,000*. Well, *that* got my attention. Even if his story was bullshit, I *wanted* to believe him. Jimmy kept so much from me."

You and me both, I judged, fuming inwardly.

"So I said I'd think about it," she went on. "But he said there wasn't any time to think. We had to act. Because the guy who could lead us right to it was here now and would be gone soon. So I asked him who that could be, and Rudert pointed at the door, said, 'The guy you just waited on, just walked out.' Meaning you, JP. I was flirty with you that first time you came into Al's because I'd heard you bought Jimmy's boat. I didn't know anything about any money. But right away I knew there was chemistry, too . . . so . . ."

Was Kelly starting to babble? I shouted, "*Goddammit!* Look at me!" Stunning us both.

She compressed her lips, turned slowly and fixed those piercing blue eyes on mine, giving me a vicious glare.

Shocked at my sudden and seething anger, I gripped the steering wheel with both hands, maybe to keep from hitting her, enraged by her deceit. Tasting bile, I rasped, "Did Rudert say where the money came from?"

"It was his uncle's money, a man named Sloan," Kelly answered with annoying calm. "'And *my* inheritance,' he said."

"And you believed him."

"What I did," she continued, her cold stare intensifying, "was ask him what I had to do for the money, and he said, 'Simple. Just keep that guy off his boat for an evening, give me time to do some salvage work.'"

Again I exploded, yelling, "The asshole said that? *Salvage?*"

"Claimed he was a 'salvage consultant,'" she said, her eyes narrowing as she leaned back against the door, folding her arms across her chest.

"Shit," I mumbled, banging the steering wheel with my palms. Asking myself: Was Rudert *another* Travis wannabe? Because I found it *unthinkable* that Rudert could consider himself a McGee-like good guy—a man out to right wrongs, help others, recover what the unlucky had lost and had no hope of finding.

"This all means something to you, right?" she said.

I had stupidly tipped my hand, and Kelly had seen it. "So our thing was just a diversion," I said, buying time to calm down, figure my options.

"How it started, maybe. Not how it ended." Those clear blue eyes, now so open and seemingly truthful, helpful.

I went mute with rage, sickened by her admitting she would sleep with a guy she barely knew on the slimmest *chance* it could lead to money. What else was she capable of? I wondered. Then her own words came back to haunt me: "I don't fuck around," she'd said. Meaning, I only fuck for a reason? A specific goal? A fair exchange?

"You gonna hit me?" she dared, reading my impulses, shocking me back to our showdown. I glared at her.

"Well, don't do it," she warned. "We need each other."

"Like hell."

"We either get out of this thing together, or we both get hurt."

Furious, I elbowed my door open and bolted from the Jeep, wanting to whale on somebody, something. I'd never felt like such a dumbshit, so foolish and used. *Betrayed.* Hell, I bet she never even was a teacher. All I had was her word. No one else had confirmed her claim.

I stormed off maybe ten steps before realizing I'd left her alone in my car, with the key in the ignition, and nearly $500,000 in cash, *my* half mil at the moment. And I knew I couldn't afford to act out now at all. Too many people were crowding the lot, milling around, taking pictures of the scenery. I didn't want to attract any witnesses, especially ones with cameras. Or cell phones. Good citizens who'd call up the cops. I took a full breath of fresh air and hurried back to the Jeep.

Climbing in, I found Kelly looking almost amused. She said, "Rudert?"

"Screw Ray Rudert!" I shot back. "Or have you done him already, too?"

"Don't be disgusting," she snapped. "Look, I'm as confused and angry as you are, okay? I don't know what's happening here anymore. But he's not going to just give up. You want him dogging you forever?"

I reverted to my cold, remote stare. I definitely did not want some dipshit punk chasing me around. Because I was accessibly real, not some indestructible fictional hero.

"How'd you find out his name?" she asked.

"We had a little scuffle on *Siren Song* and he fell overboard."

"But he's alive," she stated definitely, positively. "He just left me a message, a new number to call."

Good God, I thought. So maybe I *did* save his ass.

"We have to trust each other again," she tried. "Please tell me—"

"But there's nothing to tell," I said, cutting her off, thinking: I won't ever trust her again, not after this scene. "And there sure as hell isn't any $150,000," I added, equivocating boldly, knowing the actual amount, the whole stash just inches from her body.

She stared hard at me again and pressed her lips tightly. Was she trying to think of some new way to call me out, get me to fess up?

Then she surprised me with tears. I watched them well up and gather in the corners of her eyes, then spill and trickle slowly down her cheeks. She made no sound, no move, didn't even try to blink away her weeping. Was she so good an actress that she could cry on demand? But she wasn't hurting. She was raging now herself.

"That absolutely fucking *cannot be true!*" she hollered, her body rigid, both fists clenched. Then she struck out at me, landing a good right-cross to the side of my jaw before I could grab her arm and twist it down out of sight, afraid somebody might have noticed us arguing.

My face stinging, I tried to get control with "You're really scared, huh? Well, get a grip."

Her mouth quivering, she gave a quick nod, then said, "Let go. You're hurting me."

I slowly released my hold on her, alert for another sucker punch.

"Don't you get it?" she cried. "We've *both* been used. And this guy's crazy. And vicious. And desperate. So if he doesn't get his money . . ."

"Yeah? Then what?"

"*Please*," she begged. "If you found it, tell me."

I stared at her, watching the little scar on her cheekbone redden.

Then she seemed to cave in, give up, twisting herself around to look out the side window. Next, speaking so faintly I could barely hear her, Kelly said, "Rudert never called himself a 'salvage consultant.' I made that up."

"Aw, gimme a goddam break!" I roared, this time slamming my fists on the steering wheel. "Don't you *ever* quit?"

"Just hear me out," she said, facing me again. "That night I stayed over on the boat, I saw you were reading John D. MacDonald. I sneaked a look at the copyright page, and I knew it was one of Jimmy's, cuz he always put his initials in tiny letters at the lower lefthand corner."

A key detail I'd failed to notice over twenty times.

"So? The hell's MacDonald got to do with Rudert?" I asked, my heart racing.

"It's how MacDonald helped Jimmy to write about Sloan, that's what's important."

Her words cut through my anger, leaving me dazed, but still on guard. How much did she really know about the predicament Parnell had put me in?

"What I'm wondering now is, did you find anything else of Jimmy's with his precious books? Any writing?"

I let the silence build. I think we both realized this was a pivotal moment, a turning point for us.

"I need to hear what you know about Parnell and Sloan and all this stuff I'm supposed to have," I finally said. "And when you first knew it."

She heaved a sigh, then began: "We were living in Green Bay, and one night I was coming home from a walk and I noticed light in our basement window, the corner where Jimmy had set up a small office with a bookshelf, file cabinet, and desk. He always kept the file cabinet and desk locked because they were full of 'confidential work memos and personal records and notes.' Or so he told me. I never knew what to think."

I tried to listen carefully as Kelly went on about her tense husband, the guy always fearful that the "badasses and freaks" he hauled in were eventually going to get him.

"And when I told him to lighten up," she continued, "he would always say work was complicated, not to bug him . . ."

"Did he ever do any freelance work?" I asked. "Like a *private* detective?"

"I don't know," Kelly replied and, as if I hadn't spoken, resumed with "I went close to the basement window and peeked in. And there was Jimmy *writing*, frantically composing, like some mad genius. He was hammering away with two fingers on a little old-timey typewriter I'd never seen before. There were newspaper clippings scattered all around him, on the desk, at his feet."

Strangely, her narrative was having a calming effect on us both.

"So you surprised him and he actually *told* you all about Sloan?"

"You've seen his writing, haven't you?" she insisted, her eyes boring in on me again, her brows knit in concentration.

Self-protectively I stalled, stared off, followed the progress of a struggling parasailor in the harbor below.

Then a car door slammed on the vehicle parked next to me and I cowered.

"And you think *I'm* tense," scoffed Kelly. But now she knew it was worth her while to narrate. It seemed that Jimmy told her nothing, had put away all his papers and typewriter before she walked into the basement. But curious as she was, the next morning she discovered in a garbage bag in the garage a much torn-up early draft of a story he was calling "Champagne Shuffle." Nowhere near complete.

"It was a story about money," she said. "A lot of money. The money I'm asking you about now. The money you probably have."

"The money he took from Sloan?"

"It's on the boat, isn't it? You've got it."

Coldly, I answered, "You must think so, giving me to Rudert every chance you get. The little bastard was going to kill me for that money. And now I'm supposed to just count out the cash to you?"

"I'm broke, if you want the truth," she admitted. "Why do you think I'm waitressing? And there's no going back in the classroom, to teaching, not now. I'm a wreck. So I need money to live on, okay? Until I figure out what to do."

"And so along came Rudert promising instant wealth, and you couldn't help yourself."

She showed me a tired smile. "That's about it. That's how simple it was. A dream of easy money to buy a life of my own."

That line struck me as too well crafted, like she was being a good actress again and knew it.

"So here we are," I said. "About to commit ourselves to . . . what exactly?"

"Giving *ourselves* a break."

I asked, "Why didn't Parnell run off with the money after you guys split up? Start a new life himself someplace else?"

"He was too young. And it wasn't enough money to last forever, $150,000. And he loved his job. He was a good cop, they said."

"Good enough to find Rudert's connection."

"Rudert's connection to what?" she asked, fixing on me, looking confused.

"Somehow Parnell found out that Rudert and some girl had planned to rob Sloan the night he drove into Lake Michigan."

"Jimmy could *prove* that?"

"No one really knows. Not even Rudert, I suspect."

"How do you know Jimmy thought Rudert was involved?"

"I just know."

"But if there was any money, and it was actually Sloan's money, why would Jimmy write anything about it?" she asked.

"Maybe he felt sure no one could ever connect him to it. Maybe he needed to get everything down on paper, off his conscience. No witnesses."

"So how did Rudert ever figure out Jimmy had Sloan's money?"

"Maybe Jimmy hauled Rudert in for questioning," I suggested, hearing the cassette tape in my head. "And maybe Jimmy slipped up and said something that let Rudert know Jimmy was at Northport when Sloan died."

Then Kelly disclosed, "Rudert even tried to blackmail Jimmy. I found a ripped-up note from Rudert in with the scraps of 'Champagne Shuffle.'"

On full alert again, I asked, "How could he think that threats would work? What evidence did Rudert have on Jimmy?"

"Something. I don't know."

"You think Jimmy paid?"

"Jimmy would never let himself be blackmailed. He'd go right for Rudert's throat. Grab him up and maybe throw him off a bridge. Show him who's boss. Because Jimmy could do that, be ruthless."

"But he didn't harm Rudert. He let him hang around. Why?"

"Yeah . . . why?"

Because Parnell wanted something important from him, I nearly said. A *full confession*, a release from the nagging, crippling guilt that burdened Parnell.

"But it was Jimmy who went off the bridge," I said at last.

"And Rudert's still out there," Kelly responded. "Sneaking around. Wanting his prize."

"So now you want to pay him off? Offer the creep a buy-out?"

"How much is there?" she asked, her eyes aglow. "Cuz I know you have it all."

"Enough to cover our debts and bets." Why did I feel so sad, all of a sudden?

"What's that mean?"

I looked away, considered my options. Then I said, "I'm going to talk now, okay?" Squaring up to her, sitting tall, eyes locked on hers. "I'm going to tell you how we'll handle this. And don't say a word till I'm finished."

CHAPTER **17**

Kelly had a phone number where she could supposedly reach Rudert "anytime, 24/7." So The Plan became this: While Kelly called Rudert to set up a meeting, I would go alone to the "secret place" I'd hidden The Money (I was still reluctant to admit the cash was waiting in my Jeep). I would count out $44,650.00 and call that Sloan's grand total, then conceal it in a bag. At the meeting I'd hand it over to Rudert, telling him that this was all the cash I'd found on the boat: "Take it or leave it." Then I'd say that this was his payoff for agreeing to leave both of us alone *forever*. But given Rudert's willingness to try blackmail, I wasn't getting my hopes up.

I had assured Kelly that by shorting Rudert there'd still be enough money left to give her months of worry-free, or at least materially comfortable, living. We hadn't talked specifics about *her* total take. One handout at a time. Finally, the plan was for me to make Rudert's payoff aboard *Siren Song*, still docked at Kriel's Bay Marina. I thought I'd feel less apprehensive there with lots of other people around, even though none of them would be paying us any particular attention. None could possibly guess what was actually going down inside my modest vessel.

"You said he had a gun that other time," Kelly reminded me.

"He *had* a gun. That went overboard too."

"Like he couldn't *easily* get another?"

"We're going to be in broad daylight at a very public place. He won't shoot me till he gets the money. And once he gets the money, he can't risk shooting me or anybody else."

"I want to be with you when you give him the cash," Kelly said. "I really shouldn't let you out of my sight now. I should insist on going with you to get the money."

"You don't trust me?"

"You don't trust me." I wondered which of us was withholding the most.

"At this point, before we're definitely in the clear with Rudert and anybody else who might suddenly intrude with a claim, I think it's best for you to be innocent."

"*Innocent?*" she repeated. "You mean *ignorant,* and even *more* likely to being taken advantage of . . . again."

"What? By me?" I tried to look deeply hurt by her accusation.

"I'm not liking this part of your plan at all," she said.

"But that's how it is. I've got the cash, remember? This part has to be my call." Stated in my best commanding, pedantic tone.

"Okay. But I want to ride to the marina with you. I insist on that. I'll stay in the car, stay out of sight, if that's what you want. But I have to be there."

"Why?"

"To make sure you're safe. When I called Rudert to arrange the meeting he said he wanted to just kidnap your ass and lock you in a cellar till you gave up the loot, is how he put it. He said there were quite a few times he could've jumped you."

"Know what? Everything you've said sounds true." Being agreeable, getting under her radar.

"One other thing," said Kelly. "Rudert as much as admitted killing Jimmy."

I stared back at her, genuinely stricken. "H-how?" I stammered.

"Said he arranged for some woman friend—Kay or Shay—to lead Jimmy across Tower Drive Bridge to the Memorial Park boat landing over on the west side. They were going to put one last squeeze on Jimmy for part of Sloan's money. But when Jimmy put on his flashers, Rudert panicked, thought Jimmy was double-crossing him. He snapped, rear-ended Jimmy and took off."

"And kissed Sloan's money goodbye," I added.

"He didn't think so. He was sure Jimmy had moved anything of value aboard *Siren Song*."

"But the papers reported that Parnell's siren wasn't on. Maybe Jimmy was simply letting the woman know he was still there, following her, despite the fog."

"There's a sickening thought," said Kelly. "And that's why I want to stay close now, okay? In the background, but near you."

Then it was my turn to nod, consent to her request. She would move her car to a parking lot serving some shops across the road from the big Door County Auditorium in Fish Creek. There I would pick her up for the drive down to Sturgeon Bay. We ended by sharing a long, fierce hug, with me wondering: Which one of us is out-conning the other?

After Kelly and I had left separately from Peninsula State Park, with me exiting the way I'd come in, via the north arm of Shore Road, and after I was sure she wasn't trying to follow me, I returned to Highway 42, then drove inland on a back road, looking for some totally deserted place to park. There I would put together Rudert's payoff package. I'd be meeting him at *exactly* 3:00 p.m. That would give both Kelly and me plenty of time to get out of the county once the exchange had been made. We would need time to hide our own takes and make sure that Rudert and his posse were off our tails and out of our lives.

But even this simple plan suffered a major snag when I donned my latex gloves and flipped through the nearly half million in currency, looking for at least $44,650.00 in bills from Sloan's era, bills dated at least twenty years earlier. The problem? There weren't *any*, not one single fifty-, hundred-, or thousand-dollar bill that was more than eight years old. Which could mean what, exactly? My panicked conclusions were that 1) Parnell had successfully laundered *all* the original Sloan money and added to the grand total quite substantially and impressively by doing who-knows-what as an investor, or 2) there never really had been any Sloan money, that the rumors of Sloan's carrying around bags of cash in his gas-guzzling sedan were just that—*rumors*. Thus making *all* of Parnell's loot nothing more than scam money, ill-gotten gain. Which made me wonder—what else might he have done to assemble this small fortune? Shaken down local drug dealers? Looked the other way on criminal investigations? Fixed one helluva lot of traffic tickets? Maybe.

Then I was compelled to consider another possibility, a seemingly wild notion that now appeared obvious to me (thanks mainly to Brite). I mean, Parnell had the John D. MacDonald novels, Parnell had his *Busted Flush*–type boat, Parnell had his writing, Parnell had The Money. So couldn't Parnell actually have become a Travis McGee *for real*? Couldn't Parnell, a very *good* cop, have been so talented and restless and energetic and acquisitive that he quietly freelanced on a grand scale as a local "salvage consultant" during his off-duty hours? Maybe this pile of cash—Parnell's accumulated fees?—wasn't dirty after all, was in fact quite legit compensation for various jobs very well done. Parnell as an after-hours McGee, a closeted McGee. Why not? What proof did I have that could clearly and convincingly negate such an explanation? Especially when I had Brite's testimony to support it.

Then I remembered more proof, something I'd already seen that might confirm this suspicion. For the first time since I'd originally scanned them, I thought of the account records hidden in the false bottom of Parnell's book box. Those pages might tell me all I needed to know about Jimmy's freelance work. Even more eager now to get back to *Siren Song*, rid myself of Rudert, pull those records, and research Parnell's transactions, I turned again to the task at hand.

Meanwhile, Kelly was waiting. I had to get a move on. So I counted out the agreed-upon sum for Rudert, paying no attention whatsoever to the ages of the bills, figuring that Rudert wouldn't care about print dates once he saw the green. I wrapped the brick of cash in a small brown paper lunch sack and bound the packet with rubber bands. Whatever was going to happen would be happening soon, very soon. In fact, I had taken too much time preparing Rudert's parcel and was now running a little late. I took off in a hurry to meet Kelly in Fish Creek.

Missing the turn to the designated parking lot on my first pass-by cost us even more time. Then I had to cover the lot twice before Kelly emerged from one of the shops.

"Hey, let's hustle," I said, pushing open the door for her.

"You're the one who's late. I made a call to see if you forgot about me."

"Who'd you call? That wasn't smart," I said, getting back onto the highway and heading through, then out of town.

"I called Wally Kriel."

"Oh man . . ."

"Just drive and don't worry," said Kelly. "I pretended to be an old teaching colleague on a visit from Minneapolis."

"You give him a name?" I asked, getting anxious to sprint down the straightaway sections of the old highway that I knew were coming up. "He never forgets a name."

"No names. But it was sort of funny because Kriel said you must have been pretty popular in Minneapolis because I was the *second* teacher to call about you just today."

"Really? Did you think to ask who the first caller was?"

"Sure. It seemed like the natural thing to do, since we're all supposed to know each other from working at the same school. It was a guy named Kevin something. I forget."

Vesical.

"You know who Kriel's referring to?"

"Uh-huh. I think so. Any message?"

"This Kevin's at Hotel du Nord."

We crawled through Juddville and Egg Harbor because the tourist traffic had thickened and slowed to the point that trying to pass cars was a hopeless undertaking. I was sure that there was no way we could be at Kriel's marina and aboard *Siren Song* by 3:00 p.m. on the dot.

What happened next has to be told slowly, even though the event itself occurred in a flash. First, Kelly and I, running late, drove into Kriel's marina complex at 3:09. I happened to have noted the time in order to settle a bet with Kelly. Before I could call for my modest winnings ($1), before I'd even parked the Jeep, let alone shut off the engine, with *Siren Song* in our sights because it was still moored right where I'd left it, we both watched two people, a man and woman, the man clearly being Ray Rudert, board my boat, scout the area for witnesses, then check the time on Rudert's wristwatch. Next, they nervously, tentatively stepped toward the cabin entrance.

Rudert, taking one last look around, pulling out yet another smoke from the ever-present pack in his shirt pocket, lighting up and inhaling a deep drag, letting the glowing cigarette hang from his lips, next produced a passkey and unlocked the cabin door. When he pulled the door open and stuck his head in for a peek, an enormous air-sucking gasp and then an ear-splitting explosion sent both Rudert and the woman flying skyward where they floated raggedly for several long seconds before falling back into the splinter- and glass-filled fireball that my boat had instantly become. That vision was further fragmented by several smaller but still fierce blasts that tossed the bodies off into the channel. And suddenly my once-stable cabin cruiser became little more than a black cloud of smoking debris scattering itself over the bodies and across the waters of the boat basin.

My first words to Kelly were "Jesus God, did you see *that*?!" While my first thoughts were There goes Rudert, there goes *Siren Song*. But there goes all of Parnell's books and clip files and account records and writings as well as my notes, hidden in the case of the little Smith Corona portable. That is, I *hoped like hell* all of those documents had been destroyed because the incriminating nature of . . .

I turned to Kelly and asked abruptly, "Can you drive this?" Gesturing at my Jeep.

Wide-eyed with shock, breathing heavily through her open mouth, Kelly gave a quick nod.

"It's stick shift," I pointed out.

Kelly nodded. "I know," she finally mumbled.

"Listen, okay? Take off right now, go get some beer, bring it back as though we were about to go out for a cruise if Kriel had gotten the boat fixed. But while you're away, you've got to hide a gym bag that's right behind you on the floor. And hide this, too," I added, handing her the wrapped stack of bills that was to have been Rudert's.

Kelly accepted the bundle, nodding and nodding like a puppet.

"Now I'll run over there and holler, go a little berserk. I'm sure the cops are on their way so drive slowly. Don't get stopped for any reason. And hide those things carefully and safely. It's just you and me now. You okay with this?"

Kelly continued to nod, refusing to speak.

"Say so," I urged.

She cleared her throat, managed, "I-I'm okay. I w-won't mess up. Don't worry."

"Be careful," I said as I climbed out of the Wrangler, helped Kelly change seats. "I'm trusting you with every-thing."

"Yeah," she replied, and I hoped her dazed, sagging face was one I could trust.

I closed the door and she took off, her posture rigid, her eyes focused straight ahead.

Then for several desperate seconds, I thought to myself: You've just sent a woman you don't really trust driving off in your car with nearly half a million dollars in untrace-able and very transportable bills, a woman you may never see again. My heart began a deep slow ache.

But shouts from Wally Kriel brought me back to the painful present. I stared at the cloud of black smoke thinking: Sorry Dad, I tried, I really did, but the Endless Summer Cruise just wasn't meant to be. On the dock Kriel roared, "What the *hell*?! What in the *goddam hell*?!" He was holding his head with both hands, looking bug-eyed at me as I began my jogging approach, then aimed his gaze at the pile of smoldering flotsam that was once *Siren Song*. I hurried to meet him, knowing that we both had a helluva lot of explaining to do.

Before I could get close enough to Kriel to say anything in less than a yell, the howl of sirens filled the air as an endless parade of emergency vehicles appeared from every direction and converged on the disaster site. Police patrol cars, EMT vans, fire trucks, marine rescue launches, a local TV station's roving SUV, and gawkers. It looked as though everyone in the general area had called 911 at the moment of detonation. By now my nervous left hand had gripped and crushed my already splintered ID card. I joined Kriel at the water's edge, and the first thing I noticed was the tattered, charred remains of my dad's yellow sou'wester hat, still oddly afloat.

Among the questions I expected from Kriel, one would no doubt be, Did you smell anything suspicious when you brought the boat into the marina? I was fairly certain I'd neglected to mention the noxious fumes to Kriel, but I wasn't sure I hadn't inadvertently told somebody else. I don't think I discussed it with Kelly or Brite, and weren't they the only people I'd spoken to since leaving the boat at Kriel's? So it seemed the survivalist thing for me to do now was stonewall it on the fumes.

But what about Kriel? Had he authorized his employee Rudert to board my boat, unlock the cabin, and do an inspection? Would my supposedly good friend and mentor Wally Kriel be named liable for the death and destruction caused by my oversight? If it did come down to Kriel's being charged with anything, I was prepared to tell all in his defense, or tell at least enough to put him in the clear. I still had some vestiges of a code of conduct. And all this time the sirens continued their pulsating screams. It was like being back at Hoover High in Minneapolis with its "Synchronized-Alert Siren System Escape Enhancer." If ever I truly needed a genuine *escape enhancer*, it was right this minute.

And then I saw it, a coherent picture, a way of composing the horrific scene before me in such a way that I could live with it and myself. The blaring sirens triggered my imaginative leap, my instant creative construct. This whole disaster was RUDERT'S OWN DAMN FAULT.

As I contemplated the image of him going silently airborne again from the aft deck of *Siren Song*, I judged that he got exactly what he deserved. He was responsible for the boat's being storm-damaged in the first place. He was also responsible for my compulsive locking of every side window, hatch, and door. He was the one who couldn't wait on deck as instructed for a cash payment that would radically improve his life, that was probably a couple of years' income for him, a payment that would not have required him to open any doors to any cabins where, if you lead with your face behind a lit cigarette, you'll get instantaneous combustion, and the fate called violent death. This mess could have been averted if Rudert had simply *done as he'd been told*, been the least bit focused and patient. Like the rest of us, he'd had his own dreams, and they could have come true. Instead, Rudert confirmed the McGee claim that victims typically arrive at the wrong place at the wrong time, usually in too big a hurry.

Armed with all these self-defensive rationalizations, I walked into the circle of investigators, ready to lie my ass off, if necessary, to protect and preserve my winnings. Again, some of Kriel's words came back to both haunt and inspire me as I prepared for this critical public performance. Hadn't the wise Wally said at the start: "If you find a treasure map or a diamond ring, it's all yours," or something to that effect?

Damn straight, Wally, I concurred. Let the storifying begin.

But where was Kelly Shelberg? Where exactly was my hard-earned prize?

CHAPTER **18**

The afternoon dragged on as one investigator after another from an infinite number of agencies (including insurance) questioned me along with all the other witnessess—marina workers, boaters, tourists. The marine rescue squad retrieved the charred bodies from the channel and removed them from the area. The identities of the victims were quickly established—the man was known to be a Bay Marina employee named Raymond Rudert, although official confirmation of that fact had to be delayed until dental records supporting the finding could be located. The problem was "the guy had no ID on him, no wallet even," one of the officers reported within earshot of me. "And he supposedly always carried this really distinct billfold," the uniformed cop explained to his plainclothes superior. "Start looking for it. That could be a big help to us," answered the detective.

And my heart lurched at that because I still hadn't ditched Rudert's wallet. In fact, I'd stupidly "hidden" it in the gym bag with The Money because I wasn't able to escape *Siren Song* with more than the one satchel when Kriel was watching me.

And the woman? She was positively and legally identified as Shay Farrell, an account rep and data analyst for a local telemarketing business called Maxim Communications. My response to this revelation was a nod of acceptance, a nod of acknowledgement that Shay Farrell had probably been bait for both Sloan and Parnell. Thus making Rudert chief architect of the high-risk, no-reward scam hatched two decades earlier. But was Shay Farrell actually Rudert's backup, his *only* backup? Or were there other players still on Rudert's bumbling team? Others who would be after me, others who still believed in The Money?

After an hour passed, my dread increased tenfold. *Where was Kelly?* If she didn't return damn soon, my story about sending her out to get beer in preparation for a cruise aboard my little (hopefully repaired) yacht would lose all credibility. And the possible reasons explaining her long absence were that she had ditched my car, retrieved her own, and taken off with all the cash, once she'd found it. She could afford to go a good long way for a good long time. Why would she need me if she already had half a million? What could she see herself owing me?

Then at 4:19 p.m. my prayers were answered. Kelly returned carrying a twelve-pack of Miller Lite, looking like a girl about to go on a boating date. I stood up and hurried closer, offering to carry the beer, but really wanting to get to her before the cops. The closer I came the worse she looked. She had plastered on a big grin but it was quivery at the edges. Her face was oddly askew. She seemed fearful, numb, dazed as though she were lost in a full emotional meltdown.

"It's not the explosion," she began, answering a question I hadn't asked.

"What, then?"

"There's so *much*! I just sat staring at it, shivering like I'd been caught in a snowstorm. I couldn't stop shaking. I could hardly *breathe*. Where did it all come from?" She zeroed in on me with an unblinking stare, her expression both apprehensive and fascinated. "*Where?*" she repeated.

"It's a mystery," I answered. "Is it safe?"

"I hid everything."

"Then don't say any more about it now."

And we turned to face the gang of inquisitors anxious to find confirmation for my story and ask us both all the same questions one more time.

When Kelly and I were allowed to leave, we were still shaking, dizzied by the tower of black smoke billowing up from the torched fiberglass that once was *Siren Song*. We began stumbling toward the parking lot on our way to my Jeep, when we were intercepted by Wally Kriel, clutching his heart and struggling to draw a breath.

"God *damn*, but I'm sorry about all this, JP," he gasped. "I never had anybody free to inspect the vessel today. Crazy day. Crazy as hell now. *Unbelievable!*" he blurted, clapping his hands and looking back at where *Siren Song* should have been moored, at the black cloud it had become. Turning to me again, pulling off his glasses, he said, "You must need some place to sleep, right? You want me to hook up one of the other boats in stock? Be glad to."

"No . . . no thanks. I appreciate your help, but I'm afraid *Siren Song* was jinxed from the start."

He slowly put on his glasses and stared at us wordlessly, seeming to want Kelly to supply an explanation for what we'd all witnessed earlier, and for what I'd just said. The silence quickly became strained, so I reiterated our story of how Kelly and I planned to go out on *Siren Song* for the afternoon. I was still lugging around the crucial twelve-pack.

Kriel didn't seem to care. Instead he asked me, "Did you smell anything unusual when you brought the boat in? Like fuel or exhaust fumes?"

"Uh-uh," I answered. "Nothing unusual."

We shook hands and it was goodbye to Wally "The Deal" Kriel, still wagging his head, rubbing his palm over his heart, then fiddling with his glasses.

During the quiet and tense drive back to Fish Creek and Kelly's car, I was the first to risk conversation. I asked, "What are you thinking about?"

"My doubts. I have some *serious* doubts."

"About what?" Taking my eyes off the crowded roadway.

"I found Rudert's billfold." Staring aside.

"Uh-huh. I should've tossed it or burned it long ago. I better do that first thing now. I took it from him during our fight on the boat."

"You know what I think?" Turning her face toward me at last. Something about this exchange had a familiar ring. Her tone had suddenly become Margot's, that flat, laconic, all-business voice she used when she dismissed me from her future.

I shrugged, looked down the road, said nothing, not wanting her to go Margot's route.

"Maybe you staged the whole scene," she went on. "Set Rudert up. Lured him aboard to give him back his lost wallet, and—"

"You think I *rigged the explosion*?!" I cut in. "*Murdered him?*"

"I thought, if you were willing to do that to cut him out of this deal, what am I going to get?"

"You can't be serious."

"Then I remembered—you're just an English teacher. I'm just an English teacher. And English teachers aren't violent. They don't have the guts to do anything that horrible."

"Gutless . . ."

"It's not something we'd know about, know how to do."

"But I thought I'd killed him once already, remember? When he went overboard in the storm. And you know what? It wasn't that hard to live with."

"Don't talk that way. Just thank God it's not on you, his death. Or me either."

But it *was* on me. And the shadow of guilt was already blighting my conscience, my prospects. And the guilt was growing by the mile—the bigger the guilt, the bigger the shadow, the darker the future. I ground my teeth.

But I understood perfectly how Kelly had just defined the trauma we'd shared so *she* could live with it. My guilt wouldn't be so easily rationalized away. I changed the subject. "The money," I said. "At least that's safe, right?"

"You'll see. So the real question now is, will you share?"

"How about this? A fifty-fifty split. My property losses will be covered by insurance, and you do have a legitimate 50/50 claim."

"You bet your ass I do," she said evenly. "The best possible claim. Whatever he was up to all those nights and weekends cost me a marriage. That's how obsessive Jimmy was."

It might have been the right time to tell Kelly about Rudert's judgment of Parnell—"The guy was a bad cop, into some bad shit." But I couldn't go there. She might still harbor some illusions. Besides, it was payback time for both of us. Why ruin the moment?

"A *quarter million dollars*," she whispered, almost reverently.

"Only if you can get it out of here."

"Out of where?"

"This area. The county. The state. Go someplace where nobody's paying attention to you and then stash it in a safe deposit box."

"We can't show it around here. I understand."

"You can't create any kind of peculiar or suspicious paper trail *anywhere*. So don't put it in your savings or checking account, don't go out and buy a car or condo with cash, don't make *any* big purchases unless you pay with money orders or travelers checks. You don't want to have to explain this money to anybody."

Kelly stared back at me, looking both amazed and then amused by my lecture.

"What?" I asked, irritated that she found my instructions somehow humorous.

"I was *married* to a cop, remember? I know how these things work."

"What I'm saying is, we have to think about every move we make for a while. One careless mistake and we'll have things to explain that we can't."

That remark was met with silence . . . which lingered.

Finally, Kelly continued with, "I'm going to take at least a year off from teaching. I'm going to leave this area. You're right about needing to do that. The thought of facing another upper midwest winter is just too depressing. And I'll want to be left alone to sort things out."

"Look, you're not obligated or anything by—"

"I'm not rejecting you," she cut in, touching my fore-arm, stunning me. "I'm not saying you won't ever be in my life again. I just want to be sure what I think and why I think it."

Wishing *I* had been the one to lay out the terms, but seeing the fundamental wisdom of Kelly's perspective—that splitting up till the smoke cleared and the case closed and our heads were right would be the judicious thing to do—I said, "If that's how you want it." Struggling now to remain patient with the slow-and-go tourist traffic.

"That's how it *is*. How it has to be. For a time anyway."

I gave her a direct look, drank in the cool blue of her eyes, felt hopeful that we weren't yet through with each other. Yet, I could also imagine a day coming when we'd hurl accusations at one another, hating the secret we shared. I said, "We've got to swear total secrecy *forever* about this."

"In blood?" she kidded.

"There's already been enough blood."

"You're right. Total secrecy."

"I can count on you?"

"In lots of ways." And she leaned close and kissed me on the cheek. A goodbye kiss?

We drove the rest of the way back to her car in thought-ful silence. But when we reached the parking lot where her ancient Civic sat baking in the sun, I asked, "So where'd you hide it?"

"In the trunk of my car. I don't have a spare tire. So I put your bag in the well under the cover panel and piled it over with my stuff."

"Oh man," I said. Then, "Follow me inland."

Kelly unlocked her Civic, took a moment to check the trunk, then trailed me out to an empty stretch of roadway hidden by thick woods. Finally, once more in my Jeep, with the Nike bag on my lap, I was ready to disburse the funds.

"Hang in there," I said. "You're almost home. But I'm going back to Sturgeon Bay to calm down Kriel, finish the paperwork."

"I'm pulling out right away," she said, as if Rudert's accomplices were gathering around for a surprise attack.

"Where're you going?"

"San Francisco, I think. Eventually."

"Why California?"

"I've got a very good girlfriend there. She and her husband have just split up. She needs me and I need a place to be."

"Well, it's a good thing you'll have money. Frisco's expensive."

"You're so practical . . . I mean, at a time like this."

Was she teasing? "Gotta be tough," I answered.

She brought her left hand carefully to her cheekbone, touched the scar with her fingertips. "If you hold still," she said, "I could try again to give you one of these in about the same place."

"His and hers. Trademarks. Love wounds."

"I guess," she said, easing back, her mind already elsewhere. Her sudden coolness was startling.

I, on the other hand, was suddenly close to tears. Tears of relief, joy, affection, admiration. Kelly *was* tough. She had just declared her independence, her desire to be rid of me. And that sobering realization cut through my emotions. There had been enough tears when Margot bailed out to trade up. Then I found myself wondering what Margot would think of me now. Was a quarter mil in cash enough to get her attention? Or was that chump change in the realm she now inhabited? Maybe I'd try to find out.

Then Kelly interrupted my seconds-long reverie with "Is it time to deliver presents yet?"

"Have you been naughty or nice?" I managed.

"You show me."

So we got down to the business of counting out the cash, going our separate ways. I insisted that Kelly take a full quarter-mil cut, while I got the short stack of *only* $244,650.00. I also kept Rudert's wallet, which I would burn, pulverize, and either bury deep in the earth or scatter on the waters of Green Bay at the first opportunity.

"Aren't you scared?" she asked remotely.

"A little."

"Well, don't start snapping that ID badge. Everyone'll know."

"Broke the habit."

"Yeah? When?"

"Today."

"Cool."

Kelly's last words to me—once she had gathered, bagged, and concealed her share—were "This changes everything, JP." Spoken matter-of-factly.

Then she walked to her Civic, unlocked it, slid in, and drove off without giving me a backward glance, disappearing from my life in seconds.

CHAPTER 19

Loose ends. Loose ends. Loose ends. While seeking solace at The Wayfarer Haven—Unit 12 again—I remained spooked by my new guilt-laden wealth, my shameful involvement in the deaths of two people. Already I was obsessing about the situation, and I would dream about it repeatedly during my fitful final night in Door County.

But first—after I entered my room and sat down exhausted on the bed, desperately clutching my Nike bag of cash like a life preserver—I noticed the gleaming ship's bell that Jens had mounted on the room's front wall. Under the bell was a small brass plate on which Jens had engraved: JPG—From and For His Father. My father who had such faith in me and my integrity. What would he think of the tough new me—calculating, cool, committed to doing not the right thing, but the expedient thing?

The following morning I woke up at dawn in the gray half-light of an overcast sky, not feeling at all rested. I couldn't even make the decision to get up or stay hidden under the covers. I still had to ditch Rudert's wallet. Then

I wondered about the stolen audiocassettes—*two complete tapes.* I hoped that Rudert destroyed both to avoid being connected to Parnell. And even though Parnell himself had dared to write about the supposed crime, had left a paper trail leading me right to him, that too was obliterated, blasted away in the volcano of *Siren Song.* But Rudert, blown apart as completely as my possessions and Parnell's documents, would always be the ghost over my shoulder.

Frozen in place on the motel bed, haunted and confused by too many ethical dilemmas, I found some relief by recalling a line of advice from a text by someone other than John D. MacDonald. In Larry Watson's *Montana 1948,* the character Len McAuley tells the twelve-year-old narrator that being a peace officer in Montana means knowing when to look and when to look away.

I was ready to not just look away but *run away* from questions I no longer wanted to face. Like McGee, I was now simply trying to save myself.

So, the next move I made after shaving, showering, and donning stale and wrinkled day-old clothes (I'd lost my *entire* summer wardrobe in the boat fire) was to ring up Vesical at the Hotel du Nord in Sister Bay. Kevin always went first-class. I hoped we could get together for breakfast at Al Johnson's, after which I'd show him the sights. It was going to be a major challenge for me to perform the role of laid-back summer tour guide when all I wanted myself was to leave Door County behind me.

Vesical answered after just two rings.

I didn't know where to start, how to tell him all that had happened in the last twenty-four hours.

"The gist of it is that my boat blew up in Sturgeon Bay," I said.

"Blew up?" Vesical had that incredulous teacher's tone.

"Right at the marina. It was in for repairs."

"You mean *exploded?*"

"A total loss. And Kev, there were two fatalities. A guy who worked there and his girlfriend, I guess. It's a long story. They weren't supposed to be anywhere near the boat."

"Man-oh-man, I feel *terrible* for you. And bad about myself. I made the trip up here just to freeload a boat ride. *You* okay?"

"No, but I'd like to see you. Could be the best medicine. Especially if we *don't* talk about it." I pulled aside the motel curtains, checking out my Wrangler, my escape vehicle, and I became even more tempted to just take off.

Like a teacher reminded of hall duty, I arrived at Al Johnson's almost ten minutes *before* the scheduled meeting time, and in similar fashion Vesical had arrived even earlier, and (my God!) was engaged in conversation with none other than Nelson Brite. They were talking like old buddies, Kevin poking his forefinger into his palm, driving home a point, while Brite chuckled and nodded encouragement. I hurried up to them, prepared to deny everything. But Kevin's next remark to Brite was "I see lots of talent here. There's so much going on in this area. Did you know that some guy left the town of Washington Island enough money to build a community theater out there?"

"I read that, yes."

"Well, to a theater guy, the kind of generosity they offer around here is damn impressive. I just signed for a two-day play-judging gig in Green Bay that will be very worth my while artistically *and* financially."

Still standing next to the table, I couldn't manage to get a word in edgewise. Finally, Kevin noticed me, threw up his arms, and shook my hand with both of his. Sitting down, I began, "So you've met the conscience of the county, Mr. Nelson Brite."

Kevin showed Brite a dazzling white smile, and said, "I've been meaning to ask about a book of yours I read not too long ago." Vesical squinted heavenward in concentration, his brow furrowed, eyebrows knit. "A paperback novel," he recalled at last, zeroing in on Brite again. "A student gave it to me and said I should make it into a screenplay. 'Be a way cool mystery movie' is how he put it. Called *Repeat Business.*"

Brite nodded, glanced over at me, winked.

"I missed that one," I said. "What's it about?"

Vesical answered, "How this local cop in a resort area like this makes himself some big money by freelancing on the side. He quietly finds out about illegal deals set to go down, and then he runs his own stings to beat the bad guys out of their cash."

"What kinds of deals?" I asked.

"The gamut. All the way from drug deliveries to university dorms and area high schools, to gun buys for local street gangs, to chop-shop payoffs for car thieves, to bribe money from cooked developers. Something new every couple weeks."

"That's the plot," remarked Brite, and I fancied he winked at me again.

"And the beauty of it," Vesical said to me, "is that the cop *always* worked alone, never once told anybody anything about what he was doing, how much he made, not even his girlfriend. Just dreamed up his plans and ripped off the crooks. A real master of disguise, too, never generating any suspicion about himself."

I didn't know whether to laugh or cry. I still wasn't home free. Shit.

"I had an inside source, almost a cowriter," revealed Brite, so cool he made me wince.

"Anonymous, I suppose," said Vesical.

"Now and forever," said Brite. "Considering how things have turned out."

"What do you mean?"

Again my throat tightened. Because I knew he was somehow part of the plot, was somehow connected to Parnell's covert dealings. My chronic paranoia suddenly flared.

Brite went on, "All the copies disappeared almost immediately after publication. My source said too many people around here saw too much that was too threatening."

Meanwhile, Brite had again fixed his disconcerting gaze on me.

Then Vesical touched my arm, breaking Brite's spell, and said, "I'll send you my copy, JP. Great stuff."

"Sounds like a *must read*," I said, as wryly as I could without confusing Kevin.

"So, did you do it?" Brite asked Vesical, while still staring at me. "The adaptation?"

"You know, I made a good run at it, finished about eighty pages of script. Too many other commitments and distractions, too little free time to do what I'd like." Vesical looked off dreamily, shook his head, then added, "This is really pretty unbelievable. Actually meeting the author."

"This is a pretty unbelievable place," I muttered.

"But to answer your question directly—*no*, I haven't abandoned the adaptation, and yes, I'd love to get back into the project, especially if you could be involved." Vesical seemed to have forgotten about his old friend, me. I sat sullenly, drinking coffee, watching Brite.

"Oh, I could be *involved*," confirmed Brite, nodding. "Anything to reach my audience."

I sat there both fascinated and frightened. These two strangers seemed to understand each other almost perfectly. Panicking, I offered my apologies, lied about a scheduled meeting with insurance adjusters, then stood to leave as inconspicuously as possible. Leave before Brite got off his writing jag and started thinking seriously about me again.

But Brite stood too, saying, "Hang on, Kevin." Then to me, "I'll walk you out."

Once we were well away, Brite said, "I'm only going to ask you one question. Did you do right by her?"

I tried to hold a neutral expression. I said nothing. But somehow Brite still got his answer. Did I grimace? Half smile? Nod? I didn't think so.

Brite said, "Good man. I was right about you. For me, it's only and always about *the story*. For Jimmy it was more. He had a very special talent—he could craft scenes and schemes that only he could enact. What he did before or after those scenes ended, I didn't know and didn't want to know. We all need mystery," he declared. "Not full disclosure."

Naturally at that point, I *had* to say: "Then he did find the old man's money."

"Maybe." Brite shrugged.

"*Maybe?*"

"He never talked directly about anything." Brite gave me a look that said: *No more questions. I won't rat on you either.* Then he twitched his handlebars and winked one more time.

"One last thing," he confided. "This isn't over yet. I'm sure other people are looking, will always be looking. So pay attention. It won't be easy to keep what's yours for the moment."

And that was all. He patted my shoulder in parting, said, "Good luck, son. You'll need it." It was obvious he was anxious to get back to discussing script development with Kevin Vesical. I guess he had as much of my story as he wanted. Then I had another terrible thought: Was Kelly part of Nelson Brite's story?

In a note to Wally Kriel I told him to start looking for *another* boat for *next* summer. I thought it best to keep manufacturing options and to confirm the impression that I wasn't running away from anything or anybody. I had instructed the claims adjuster from the company insuring *Siren Song* to send the check for damages to my Twin Cities apartment. I didn't plan a long stay there because all I needed to do was 1) make sure my request for an unpaid leave of absence for the coming year from Hoover High had been duly processed and approved, keeping that door slightly ajar, that option open; 2) inform my landlord that I definitely would not be renewing my lease when it expired at the end of the month; and 3) maybe, just maybe look up Margot again. I wondered how she would react if I approached her. Certainly she would realize she wasn't talking to the complacent civil servant I was when we parted. Maybe we actually could reconnect. Money can build lots of bridges.

I would purchase a sedan (probably late model, used) that was well equipped, economical to operate, but totally nondescript, unobtrusive, not even close to being among the top five cars most often stolen for parts.

And to further ease my conscience, I would send anonymous donations to Erin Chilton (EC) and Gina Sebring (Parnell's sister), both fading fast.

I left Door County the way I'd arrived, by crossing the immense and intimidating Tower Drive Bridge in Green Bay. And like the afternoon when I first started my chaotic ordeal, the morning I departed had turned from overcast and gray to misty and foggy. Again, I was hanging close to the centerline, driving in the fast lane that wasn't moving all that fast, when I was jarred from my daydreaming and future-planning right at the peak of the arcing bridge by a Green Bay police cruiser—lightbar flashers awhirl on its roof—that came up close behind me, putting my heart in my throat. Nelson Brite *hadn't* kept silent about my complex scheming after all. I signaled and changed lanes, heading for the road shoulder on the outside edge of the bridge, wondering what I'd have to deny. But the police car wasn't after me. Instead it floated by, lights still aflash but its siren silent, hurrying off into the distance.

I thought about that other cop, Jimmy Parnell, JP, clearly my alter ego. We both fancied Travis McGee, we both had problems with personal relationships, we both were drawn into affairs that were not strictly legal. We loved boats, even if the one we both settled on was doomed. We both were involved with the same woman, the same crooks. Then I remembered Parnell's drawn, tired face that night on the Tower Drive Bridge, his expression marked by a bleak awareness of the hell about to welcome him. I had since seen that same face whenever I looked in a mirror. Had I now fully exchanged my life for his?

As I cleared the bridge, though, I impulsively decided not to follow my Highway 29 escape route west across Wisconsin, but to head south, working my way back to the Lake Michigan shoreline. Minneapolis could wait for a few hours. I wanted to visit my parents' graves, tell my dad that like Odysseus, it would be many years before I found my way home again, if ever. Tell him how I'd permanently crossed certain borders of experience, and would never again know that midwest innocence he'd worked so hard to protect. Maybe point out that shadow cloud of guilt darkening all my thoughts and deeds. I wondered if he could still accept me, let alone approve of my choices. I would ask him not to judge, but to understand. And to be with me during my endless travels and trials. Because let's face it—I'd already had more than enough danger and excitement for one summer. So I planned to head far south now, to siesta land, to slow-motion country.

But as I sped down the highway, I began thinking about Margot again, wondering how hot she'd be about a visit to south Florida in late July.